NEW GEPT

新制全民英檢

10回試題完全掌握最新內容與趨勢！

中級 聽力 & 閱讀 題庫大全

—○ 題本+解答 ○—

全MP3一次下載

9789864543120.zip

iOS系統請升級至 iOS13後再行下載，下載前請先安裝ZIP解壓縮程式或APP，
此為大型檔案，建議使用 Wifi 連線下載，以免占用流量，並確認連線狀況，以利下載順暢。

CONTENTS

目錄

NEW GEPT
新制全民英檢中級聽力 & 閱讀題庫大全

聽力測驗 答對題數與分數對照表

答對題數	分數	答對題數	分數
35	120	17	58
34	117	16	55
33	113	15	51
32	110	14	48
31	106	13	45
30	103	12	41
29	99	11	38
28	96	10	34
27	93	9	31
26	89	8	27
25	86	7	24
24	82	6	21
23	79	5	17
22	75	4	14
21	72	3	10
20	69	2	7
19	65	1	3
18	62		

閱讀測驗 答對題數與分數對照表

答對題數	分數	答對題數	分數
35	120	17	58
34	117	16	55
33	113	15	51
32	110	14	48
31	106	13	45
30	103	12	41
29	99	11	38
28	96	10	34
27	93	9	31
26	89	8	27
25	86	7	24
24	82	6	21
23	79	5	17
22	75	4	14
21	72	3	10
20	69	2	7
19	65	1	3
18	62		

TEST 01

GEPT
全民英檢

中級初試

題目本

本測驗分四部分,全為四選一之選擇題,共 35 題,作答時間約 30 分鐘。

第一部分：看圖辨義

共 5 題,試題冊上有數幅圖畫,每一圖畫有 1~3 個描述該圖的題目,每題請聽光碟放音機播出題目以及四個英語敘述之後,選出與所看到的圖畫最相符的答案,每題只播出一遍。

例:（看）

（聽）

Look at the picture. What is the woman doing?

A. She is looking at a sculpture.

B. She is appreciating a painting.

C. She is picking up a handbag.

D. She is entering a museum.

正確答案為 B。

聽力測驗第一部分自本頁開始。

A. Question 1

第1回

第2回

第3回

第4回

第5回

第6回

第7回

第8回

第9回

第10回

B. Questions 2 and 3

↑ Duty Free Shop   → Baggage Claim

← Visa Office   → Immigration

↪ Transfer

C. Questions 4 and 5

Let's Celebrate Christmas!

Santa Claus Appearance

Free gifts for
the first 100 children every time!
7 & 9 p.m. on selected Saturdays

| Dec. 2 | Dec. 9 | Dec. 16 | Dec. 23 |

Make a Wish & Decorate the Tree

Scan the QR code and see things come to life
on your mobile screen! In this AR experience,
you can enter your wish and see what kind of
decoration it turns into on our Christmas tree.
Try it for free!

SAGA Department Store | Taipei

第二部分：問答

共 10 題，每題請聽光碟放音機播出一英語問句或直述句之後，從試題冊上 A、B、C、D 四個回答或回應中，選出一個最適合者作答。每題只播出一遍。

例： （聽）Now that we've come to Kenting, we should try water sports.
　　（看）A. You can try harder next time.
　　　　　B. Yes. I'm on the way there.
　　　　　C. That sounds exciting to me.
　　　　　D. We are coming in an hour.

正確答案為 C。

6. A. You can request for a hearing test.
　 B. There are various types of noise.
　 C. You should inform them politely.
　 D. Tell them to lower their voice.

7. A. There is a bakery nearby.
　 B. Turn on the air conditioner, then.
　 C. If I were you, I'd change the recipe.
　 D. Fortunately, no one cares.

8. A. Yes. It is recognized for its technology.
　 B. Yes. Big data is efficient and helpful.
　 C. No. They're not supported by evidence.
　 D. No. There was no notice in advance.

9. A. It continues for six months.
　 B. Good things won't last forever.
　 C. The game itself is forty-eight minutes.
　 D. Some games have longer break time.

10. A. It's the best smart television.
　　B. I run a YouTube channel.
　　C. Managing a service isn't easy.
　　D. Actually, I don't use any one.

11.　A.　Which horror movie do you like best?
　　　B.　You can join online communities.
　　　C.　Change your thoughts about movies.
　　　D.　Turn right there and you'll see it.

12.　A.　What degree did you receive?
　　　B.　What inspires you to keep learning?
　　　C.　You must speak Japanese very well.
　　　D.　It's really hard to get into college.

13.　A.　Certainly. It takes four weeks to make.
　　　B.　Every woman dreams of having one.
　　　C.　You can order any dish on the menu.
　　　D.　It does not suit every person.

14.　A.　It doesn't matter which team wins.
　　　B.　How can I apply for it?
　　　C.　Wow! How lucky she is!
　　　D.　I'm curious how beautiful they are.

15.　A.　No. We have to meet on the Internet.
　　　B.　No. There isn't any special offer.
　　　C.　Yes. It's convenient to shop online.
　　　D.　Yes. They are more flexible for me.

第三部分：簡短對話

共 10 題，每題請聽光碟放音機播出一段對話及一個相關的問題後，從試題冊上 A、B、C、D 四個選項中選出一個最適合者作答。每段對話及問題只播出一遍。

例：（聽）（Woman） Excuse me. Does the next train go to the airport?

（Man） No. Actually, this is the high speed rail station. You should go to the airport MRT station nearby to get to the airport.

（Woman） Thank you for letting me know. This is my first time taking a train to the airport, so I didn't notice that.

Question: What happened to the woman?

（看）A. She missed her train.
　　　B. She got on the wrong train.
　　　C. She went to the wrong station.
　　　D. Her flight has already left.

正確答案為 C。

16. A. Chatting on the phone.
　　B. Playing an online game.
　　C. Having a web conference.
　　D. Fixing the Internet connection.

17. A. Higher housing expense.
　　B. Longer rental contract.
　　C. Rising product prices.
　　D. The trouble of moving.

18. A. He stayed up watching dramas.
　　B. He worked late at night.
　　C. He just shifted to a new job.
　　D. He has been too nervous.

19. A. The woman will check the laptop.
　　B. The woman will keep the laptop.
　　C. The man will give a presentation.
　　D. The man will take back the laptop.

20. A. The business of a company.
　　B. Building construction.
　　C. Interior decoration.
　　D. A relative.

21. A. He exercises every day.
    B. He is a member of the gym.
    C. He can learn yoga for free tomorrow.
    D. He will register for the yoga course.

22. A. Cocktail party.
    B. Costume party.
    C. Fashion party.
    D. Business dinner party.

23. A. Finding sponsors.
    B. Planning events.
    C. Inviting participants.
    D. Keeping records of the money.

24.

Photo-Editing Apps

	Picazzo	SnapPeel	Camphor	VFace
Landscape Editing	●	●	●	
Human Portrait Editing	●			●
Pricing	$12.99 per month	$11.99 per month	Free	Free

A. Picazzo.
B. SnapPeel.
C. Camphor.
D. VFace.

25.

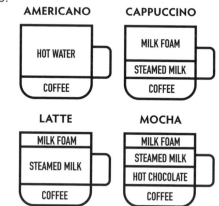

A. Americano.
B. Cappuccino.
C. Latte.
D. Mocha.

第四部分：簡短談話

共 10 題，每題請聽光碟放音機播出一段談話及一個相關的問題後，從試題冊上 A、B、C、D 四個選項中選出一個最適合者作答。每段談話及問題只播出一遍。

例：（聽）Teenagers can easily feel hurt in their social lives. When they have difficulty making friends, they may feel worried about going to school. Even if they are popular at school, they may be persuaded to do things they don't like, such as smoking or drinking, under peer pressure. The stress of fitting in can eventually make them mentally ill.

Question: According to the speaker, what makes a teenager try smoking even though they are not interested?

（看）A. Parents' complaint.
B. Friends' persuasion.
C. Romantic relationship.
D. Academic pressure.

正確答案為 B。

26. A. Reducing energy waste.
    B. Choosing energy-efficient devices.
    C. Having an economical lifestyle.
    D. Eliminating environmental pollution.

27. A. The plane will take off.
    B. The plane will arrive at Paris.
    C. Passengers will get drinks.
    D. The crew will get on the plane.

28. A. Voting age.
    B. Generation gap.
    C. Medical research.
    D. Qualification for being elected.

29. A. He should swim faster.
    B. He is good at flying a plane.
    C. He won the race by chance.
    D. He is an outstanding swimmer.

30. A. It takes place on the street.
    B. Musicians and dancers will perform together.
    C. People must sit on assigned seats.
    D. It is free to attend.

31. A. They will have to pay a fee.
    B. They will be locked in the store.
    C. It will not be possible to check out.
    D. Using the front door will be prohibited.

32. A. She will see a dentist tomorrow morning.
    B. She has never seen a dentist.
    C. She has her own insurance.
    D. She is Kevin's daughter.

33. A. A horse farm.
    B. An amusement park.
    C. A department store.
    D. A performance hall.

34.

TYPES OF BONE FRACTURE

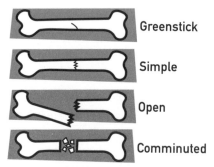

Greenstick

Simple

Open

Comminuted

    A. Greenstick fracture.
    B. Simple fracture.
    C. Open fracture.
    D. Comminuted fracture.

35. **BPS's First Online Concert**
    "Hero's Journey"

Taipei	Paris	New York	Los Angeles
7 a.m.	11 p.m.	6 p.m.	3 p.m.
Nov. 2	Nov. 1	Nov. 1	Nov. 1
Saturday	Friday	Friday	Friday

Ticket open @ bpsonlineconcert.com
$30 per person
Get a ticket and stream live worldwide!

    A. Taipei.
    B. Paris.
    C. New York.
    D. Los Angeles.

本測驗分三部分，全為四選一之選擇題，共 35 題，作答時間 45 分鐘。

第一部分：詞彙

共 10 題，每題含一個空格。請由試題冊上的四個選項中選出最適合題意的字或詞作答。

1. _____ people are expected to donate their fortune to charities rather than just buying luxury goods for themselves.
   A. Ambitious
   B. Graceful
   C. Productive
   D. Wealthy

2. _____ popular belief that he is stingy, Mr. Johnson actually lends money to his friends in need.
   A. Contrary to
   B. Surprised at
   C. In addition to
   D. Speaking of

3. The new president's approval rating declined because he has difficulty _____ his campaign promises.
   A. abandoning
   B. restricting
   C. implementing
   D. foreseeing

4. When a boss _____ their power to bully certain employees, they can create fear among the staff and make them less productive.
   A. conceals
   B. evaluates
   C. abuses
   D. surrenders

5. It was not until he _____ his identity to me that I knew he was a famous radio host.
   A. faked
   B. revealed
   C. exploited
   D. analyzed

6. The internet security software identifies _____ threats and prevent them from happening.
   A. liberal   B. mutual
   C. potential   D. conservative

7. We must _____ the whole article to ensure there is not any spelling mistake.
   A. go through   B. skim over
   C. hold on to   D. put up with

8. You need to take a rest once in a while. _____, you may burn out and collapse in the end.
   A. Nonetheless   B. Absolutely
   C. Furthermore   D. Otherwise

9. A bird can use its _____ to gather food, feed its babies or clean itself.
   A. beak   B. crown
   C. feather   D. poultry

10. There has been a _____ increase in the population in urban areas, resulting in extremely high demand for housing and public transportation.
    A. slight   B. glorious
    C. tolerable   D. significant

第二部分：段落填空

共 10 題，包括二個段落，每個段落各含 5 個空格。請由試題冊上四個選項中選出最適合題意的字或詞作答。

Questions 11-15

The James Webb Space Telescope (JWST, also known as "Webb") is the largest and most powerful space telescope ever built. It __(11)__ James Webb, who led the Apollo Program—the __(12)__ to land the first humans on the Moon.

"Webb" has special cameras designed to __(13)__ in the dust of space. The cameras are able to __(14)__ the heat radiation given off by hidden objects in space through the dust. __(15)__ "Webb", it is possible for scientists to observe the formation of stars and planets, as well as monitor the weather conditions on the planets and their moons.

11. A. was named after
    B. served as
    C. resulted from
    D. comes along with

12. A. resolution
    B. limitation
    C. strategy
    D. mission

13. A. remain crystal-clear
    B. capture images of objects
    C. find non-human beings
    D. travel here and there

14. A. trap
    B. detect
    C. inherit
    D. retrieve

15. A. Thanks to
    B. Contrary to
    C. According to
    D. In addition to

第 1 回
第 2 回
第 3 回
第 4 回
第 5 回
第 6 回
第 7 回
第 8 回
第 9 回
第 10 回

Questions 16-20

The output and consumption of palm oil saw __(16)__ growth in recent years. Therefore, some tropical countries, such as Indonesia and Malaysia, made a __(17)__ by cultivating palm trees. The economic growth brought by palm oil production, however, __(18)__ . In order to plant more palm trees, farmers have burnt vast areas of forests, which are home to many __(19)__ species, such as the orangutan. Its populations have declined by at least 25% over the past 10 years. Oil palm farming also __(20)__ climate change because palm trees release more carbon into the atmosphere than natural forests do.

16. A. rapid
    B. hasty
    C. eager
    D. vague

17. A. decision
    B. fortune
    C. difference
    D. comeback

18. A. is not without consequences
    B. can be seen as an achievement
    C. has been declining recently
    D. leads to a wealth gap between people

19. A. emergency
    B. endangered
    C. enhancing
    D. environmental

20. A. contributes to
    B. allows for
    C. deals with
    D. stems from

第三部分：閱讀理解

共 15 題，包括數篇短文，每篇短文後有 2~4 個相關問題。請由試題冊上四個選項中選出最適合者作答。

Questions 21-22

The chance of a lifetime

The biggest meteor shower of this year will be active from August 3rd through 14th, with the peak occurring around August 10th. It is expected to produce 100 to 150 shooting stars visible to the naked eye per hour. From August 7th to 13th, watch parties will be held every night in City Park. Several volunteer teachers will teach participants how to see the shooting stars using a telescope. To make a free reservation, please visit the community center's website at EPTcommunitycenter.org.

---

21. What is the main purpose of this passage?
    A. To report a discovery about space
    B. To provide details about a new star
    C. To announce an educational event
    D. To invite people to a social gathering

22. Which of the following statement about the parties is true?
    A. Entrance fee will be required.
    B. Attendees have to bring their own telescopes.
    C. They are held by some teachers.
    D. They will be held daily for a week.

第1回
第2回
第3回
第4回
第5回
第6回
第7回
第8回
第9回
第10回

Workshop on Future Technologies

Dear all,

All instructors of our university are invited to register for the workshop on future technologies. The aim of this event is to improve your understanding of groundbreaking technological inventions and their applications in industries. In the five-day workshop, you will learn from experts in a variety of fields, such as cloud computing, artificial intelligence, internet of things (IoT), etc. Moreover, you can bring a friend or family member above 12 with you. We look forward to seeing you at the workshop!

Registration Form

Name: _____   Phone: _____

Email: _____

Are you bringing a guest? ☐Yes   ☐No   Guest's name: _____

Choose the session(s) you will attend:

☐Feburary 20: Cloud computing

☐Feburary 21: Artificial intelligence

☐Feburary 22: Virtual reality

☐Feburary 23: Block chain

☐Feburary 24: Internet of things (IoT)

*All the sessions run from 7 to 9 p.m. in Meeting Room 3

23. What is the purpose of the workshop?
    A. To update students with latest trends
    B. To provide some in-house training
    C. To hire experts as university instructors
    D. To encourage technological inventions

24. According to the announcement, what is true about the workshop?
    A. It lasts for five whole days.
    B. Only instructors of the university can attend it.
    C. Participants can choose which topics they want to learn about.
    D. Registration fee varies depending on the number of sessions selected.

25. Who is most likely to speak at the workshop?
    A. A graphic designer for websites
    B. A computer maintenance technician
    C. A developer of smart devices
    D. The human resource officer of the university

第1回
第2回
第3回
第4回
第5回
第6回
第7回
第8回
第9回
第10回

Questions 26-28 are based on information provided in the following form and email.

Global Village Steak House
Customer Satisfaction Survey

Thank you for dining with us! Let us know your thoughts about our food and service by filling out this form.

Date of Visit: Oct. 29, 2023   ☐Lunch ■Dinner

Food	■Excellent	☐Good	☐Fair	☐Poor
Service	☐Excellent	☐Good	☐Fair	■Poor
Environment	☐Excellent	☐Good	■Fair	☐Poor

Your comment

My wife and I come here to celebrate our 23rd anniversary. We are impressed by your affordable prices and delicious steaks, but we waited for over 30 minutes before our food was served. The staff just kept us waiting without giving any explanation.

Name: Robert Smith   ■Male ☐Female
Age: 53   **Email:** robert99@ggmail.com

From:	manager@globalvillagesteakhouse.com
To:	robert99@ggmail.com
Subject:	Apologies from Global Village Steak House

Dear Mr. Robert Smith,

I'm sorry for the inconvenience you experienced in our restaurant last month, and I appreciate that you brought the issue to our attention. Our top priority is training staff to be caring and helpful, so we take your opinion very seriously. Your feedback will help us improve the quality of our service.

To express our regret, we would like to offer each of you a free appetizer on your next visit. You can enjoy it along with our 23rd anniversary special, which will be available next month. Thank you for your understanding, and we look forward to welcoming you back to our restaurant soon.

Yours sincerely,

Jeremy Lamb
Manager
Global Village Steak House

26. According to the form, what is true about Robert?
    A. He was surprised by the restaurant's unreasonable prices.
    B. He was not satisfied with how the staff treated him and his wife.
    C. He and his wife waited for half an hour before entering the restaurant.
    D. He got married 53 years ago.

27. What can we infer about Global Village Steak House?
    A. It is only open for dinner service.
    B. It offers a free meal to unsatisfied customers.
    C. It opened its doors in the year when Robert got married.
    D. It is now celebrating its anniversary.

28. What does Jeremy suggest he will do in the email?
    A. Ask Robert to provide more details of his experience
    B. Hire more staff for the restaurant
    C. Remind the staff to pay more attention to their service
    D. Welcome Robert in person when he comes to the restaurant

第1回
第2回
第3回
第4回
第5回
第6回
第7回
第8回
第9回
第10回

Questions 29-31

The number of electric vehicles has been increasing rapidly in recent years. There are numerous reasons that more and more people choose electric cars instead of gasoline-powered ones. First, since they run on electricity, it is possible for their owners to charge them at home and avoid the hassle of visiting a gas station. Second, unlike traditional cars that use gasoline engines, electric cars require less maintenance, and they are smoother, quieter, and easier to drive. Moreover, governments offer tax credits or subsidies to people who buy electric cars, making them more affordable than before.

While electric cars are seen as the future of automobiles, there are still some challenges to overcome. For example, it takes several hours to fully charge an electric car at home, and there is still a lack of charging spots in rural areas. Additionally, despite incentives provided by governments and recent price cuts, electric cars still cost more to purchase.

As manufacturers and governments keep addressing these disadvantages, however, more customers are expected to embrace electric vehicles. Also, in an effort to eliminate carbon emission, many governments have decided to ban conventional gasoline-powered vehicles in the future, which is likely to further increase demand for electric cars.

29. Which of the following is **NOT** an advantage of electric cars?
    A. Possibility of charging at home
    B. Less work needed to keep them in good condition
    C. Better driving experience
    D. Lower prices than gasoline-powered cars

30. In which case can it be difficult to use an electric car as a mode of transportation?
    A. Commuting to and from work
    B. Going shopping in the downtown area
    C. Picking someone up at their home
    D. Traveling the countryside for a week

31. What is mentioned as a way for governments to encourage buying electric cars?
    A. Providing financial support
    B. Forcing manufacturers to cut prices
    C. Raising taxes on traditional car owners
    D. Lowering prices of electricity

第1回
第2回
第3回
第4回
第5回
第6回
第7回
第8回
第9回
第10回

Questions 32-35

Streaming services have changed the way we watch TV. Instead of waiting for a program to be on air at a specific time, we can now watch any episode of a show whenever we want. Such convenience, however, has given rise to a new problem: "binge-watching", meaning watching multiple episodes of a show in a single sitting or over a short period of time. The term "binge" refers to the situation of doing something in an extreme way, such as overeating or overdrinking, so calling someone a "binge-watcher" also implies that they cannot control their behavior of consuming video content non-stop.

There is a psychological factor that leads to binge-watching. When we watch a TV show, the brain releases dopamine (多巴胺), which makes us feel happy. To keep this positive feeling going, we may continue to watch episode after episode, leading to binge-watching behavior. However, the longer we keep watching, the higher our tolerance becomes to the dopamine release, which means we may feel less excited in the end or even depressed when we stop.

Besides the negative impact on our mood, binge-watching can also have physical and social consequences. Sitting for long periods of time watching TV can lead to weight gain and other health problems, and it can also decrease our time for social activities and negatively affect our relationships as a result. Therefore, it is important to strike a balance between screen time and other activities.

32. What does the term "binge-watching" indicate?
    A. Watching a single episode at a time
    B. Watching TV without self control
    C. Being extremely critical when watching TV
    D. Overeating or overdrinking when watching TV

33. In what way do streaming services make binge-watching possible?
    A. They show the time a user spends on watching TV.
    B. They reward binge-watchers with special offers.
    C. They provide all episodes of a show online.
    D. They create rest time between episodes.

34. What is true about dopamine?
    A. It is the result of happy feelings.
    B. Its effect lasts for a long time.
    C. Its effect becomes weaker when we watch TV continuously.
    D. Too much dopamine can lead to depression.

35. What is **NOT** a negative effect of binge-watching?
    A. Depression
    B. Overthinking
    C. Overweight
    D. Social isolation

第1回
第2回
第3回
第4回
第5回
第6回
第7回
第8回
第9回
第10回

TEST 02

GEPT
全民英檢
中級初試

題目本

本測驗分四部分，全為四選一之選擇題，共 35 題，作答時間約 30 分鐘。

第一部分：看圖辨義

共 5 題，試題冊上有數幅圖畫，每一圖畫有 1~3 個描述該圖的題目，每題請聽光碟放音機播出題目以及四個英語敘述之後，選出與所看到的圖畫最相符的答案，每題只播出一遍。

例：（看）

（聽）

Look at the picture. What is the woman doing?

A. She is looking at a sculpture.

B. She is appreciating a painting.

C. She is picking up a handbag.

D. She is entering a museum.

正確答案為 B。

聽力測驗第一部分自本頁開始。

A. <u>Question 1</u>

SUMMER BASEBALL CAMP

9AM - 4PM
August 20-24
At TPEG Stadium

FREE
Boys & Girls
Ages 6-12

If you love baseball, join us!
In the summer camp, you will:
- Learn basic pitching skill
- Learn basic batting skill
- Participate in practice/games

For more information:
☎1234-5678 / bbcamp@littleathle.com

第1回
第2回
第3回
第4回
第5回
第6回
第7回
第8回
第9回
第10回

B. Questions 2 and 3

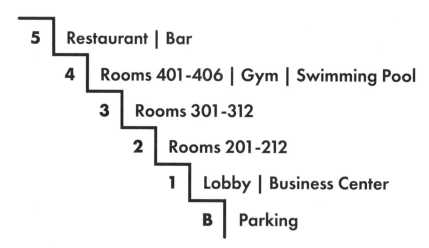

FASHION × FOOD × MUSIC
Second-Hand Clothes Flea Market

✓ Open-air café
✓ Live band performance by **JUNE DAY**
✓ Chance to win an Eye-Phone for all attendees

September 22 (Sat.) and 23 (Sun.)
1 p.m. to 8 p.m.

C. Questions 4 and 5

5	Restaurant | Bar
4	Rooms 401-406 | Gym | Swimming Pool
3	Rooms 301-312
2	Rooms 201-212
1	Lobby | Business Center
B	Parking

第二部分：問答

共 10 題，每題請聽光碟放音機播出一英語問句或直述句之後，從試題冊上 A、B、C、D 四個回答或回應中，選出一個最適合者作答。每題只播出一遍。

例： （聽）Now that we've come to Kenting, we should try water sports.
  （看）A. You can try harder next time.
    B. Yes. I'm on the way there.
    C. That sounds exciting to me.
    D. We are coming in an hour.

正確答案為 C。

6. A. It is my favorite class.
   B. I had a bad headache.
   C. The English teacher is boring.
   D. No, I usually walk to school.

7. A. I'm sorry to hear that.
   B. Sure, I passed it.
   C. Your parents will praise you, right?
   D. It's on next Friday.

8. A. No, they didn't get hurt.
   B. Yes, he is a careful driver.
   C. No, that's my dad's car.
   D. Yes, some people are there to help.

9. A. All credit to his dance teacher.
   B. Practice makes perfect.
   C. I'd say he has the talent.
   D. It's all because of their teamwork.

10. A. I'm just a few minutes away.
    B. I'll be more careful next time.
    C. He's on his way to the station.
    D. I thought you'd be on time.

第1回
第2回
第3回
第4回
第5回
第6回
第7回
第8回
第9回
第10回

11. A. I'm going to eat some popcorn.
    B. How about the bus stop nearby?
    C. 20 minutes before the movie starts.
    D. At the meeting in Miami.

12. A. Oh, what a pity!
    B. Is holding a wedding expensive?
    C. How long did you stay there?
    D. Does your room have ocean view?

13. A. They drive me crazy every day!
    B. Fortunately, they're all born healthy.
    C. We watch our spending on them.
    D. Nothing's better than regular exercise.

14. A. Did you give him some suggestions?
    B. I don't think his mother will like it.
    C. It can be a life-changing choice.
    D. His mother bought him a new bike.

15. A. Yes, I put it there.
    B. Tom was playing around there.
    C. I don't like the pattern on it.
    D. I poured too much water in it.

第三部分：簡短對話

共 10 題，每題請聽光碟放音機播出一段對話及一個相關的問題後，從試題冊上 A、B、C、D 四個選項中選出一個最適合者作答。每段對話及問題只播出一遍。

例：（聽）（Woman）Excuse me. Does the next train go to the airport?

（Man） No. Actually, this is the high speed rail station. You should go to the airport MRT station nearby to get to the airport.

（Woman）Thank you for letting me know. This is my first time taking a train to the airport, so I didn't notice that.

Question: What happened to the woman?

（看）A. She missed her train.
B. She got on the wrong train.
C. She went to the wrong station.
D. Her flight has already left.

正確答案為 C。

16. A. Having some food at home.
    B. Storing drinking water.
    C. Preparing a flashlight.
    D. Putting tapes on windows.

17. A. Have a barbecue party.
    B. Gather with the woman's family.
    C. Buy an electric griddle.
    D. Build a fire.

18. A. The yellow blouse.
    B. The white blouse.
    C. The blue dress.
    D. Both of the blouses.

19. A. He has to sort the trash.
    B. He hates going outside.
    C. He wants to protect the environment.
    D. Garbage trucks come on different days.

20. A. He caught a disease.
    B. He drove carelessly.
    C. He was hit on the road.
    D. A repair shop damaged his bike.

21. A. Having an interview.
    B. Talking about business.
    C. Reviewing a movie.
    D. Discussing in class.

22. A. The room is a mess.
    B. The man keeps watching TV.
    C. The man does not keep his promise.
    D. The man carries nothing with him.

23. A. A receptionist.
    B. A travel agent.
    C. A tour guide.
    D. A chocolate shop clerk.

24.

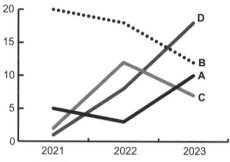

Birth Rates from 2021 to 2023
(births per 1,000 people)

A. City A.
B. City B.
C. City C.
D. City D.

25.

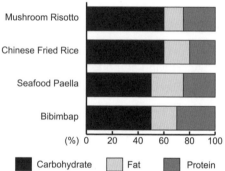

A. Mushroom risotto.
B. Chinese fried rice.
C. Seafood paella.
D. Bibimbap.

第四部分：簡短談話

共 10 題，每題請聽光碟放音機播出一段談話及一個相關的問題後，從試題冊上 A、B、C、D 四個選項中選出一個最適合者作答。每段談話及問題只播出一遍。

例： （聽） Teenagers can easily feel hurt in their social lives. When they have difficulty making friends, they may feel worried about going to school. Even if they are popular at school, they may be persuaded to do things they don't like, such as smoking or drinking, under peer pressure. The stress of fitting in can eventually make them mentally ill.

Question: According to the speaker, what makes a teenager try smoking even though they are not interested?

（看） A. Parents' complaint.
B. Friends' persuasion.
C. Romantic relationship.
D. Academic pressure.

正確答案為 B。

26. A. She forgot she'll meet Emily.
    B. She missed a deadline.
    C. She forgot to write a report.
    D. She has to finish a report.

27. A. He is a freshman in college.
    B. He does not like the south.
    C. It is warmer in his hometown.
    D. He experienced a culture shock.

28. A. Weather report.
    B. Balanced diet.
    C. Medical research.
    D. Disease prevention.

29. A. They were classmates.
    B. They were teacher and student.
    C. They were colleagues.
    D. They were doctor and patient.

30. A. Toothpaste.
    B. Diet pill.
    C. Air freshener.
    D. Skin whitening cream.

31. A. Her dog may die soon.
    B. It is easier to keep a cat.
    C. She likes cats better than dogs.
    D. She wants to find her dog a friend.

32. A. A pilot.
    B. A waiter.
    C. A travel agent.
    D. A flight attendant.

33. A. It is due before the final exam.
    B. There are several projects to do.
    C. Half of the grade is determined by it.
    D. Everyone should do it independently.

35.

W Restaurant / September

Sun.	Mon.	Tue.	Wed.	Thu.	Fri.	Sat.
				1	2	3
4	5	6	7	8	9	10
11	12	13	14	15	16	17
18	19	20	21	22	23	24
25	26	27	28	29	30	

Open 5 to 8 p.m. (weekday) /
12 to 9 p.m. (weekend)
☐ : Available ▣ : Fully booked

A. On September 7.
B. On September 11.
C. On September 18.
D. On September 19.

34.

Post Office	Bakery	Police Station
Supermarket	Public Square	Hospital
High School	Bank	Park HOME

A. At the police station.
B. At the post office.
C. At the high school.
D. At the bank.

本測驗分三部分，全為四選一之選擇題，共 35 題，作答時間 45 分鐘。

第一部分：詞彙

共 10 題，每題含一個空格。請由試題冊上的四個選項中選出最適合題意的字或詞作答。

1. The engineer found the software program did not work properly, so he _____ the settings to fix the problem.
   A. adopted
   B. adjusted
   C. accepted
   D. attended

2. If you _____ being rude to others, no one will want to be your friend.
   A. end up
   B. put off
   C. give up
   D. keep on

3. Socially active students like to _____ in various clubs and make new friends.
   A. observe
   B. surrender
   C. participate
   D. concentrate

4. Elder people with mobility issues may have difficulty getting on and off the _____ while it is moving at high speed.
   A. vehicle
   B. elevator
   C. staircase
   D. escalator

5. A recent survey shows that the _____ of voters are not satisfied with the current government, suggesting that the governing party will lose the election.
   A. authority
   B. majority
   C. minority
   D. priority

6. To be _____ adult, you should make decisions carefully and take responsibility for your actions.
   A. a radical
   B. a mature
   C. an ancient
   D. an experienced

第1回 第2回 第3回 第4回 第5回 第6回 第7回 第8回 第9回 第10回

7. The landslide resulting from the severe typhoon caused _____ damage to the mountain villages.

   A. competitive   B. comparative

   C. countable   D. considerable

8. The two parties reached an agreement on the terms and conditions of their contract after several months of _____ .

   A. recognition   B. negotiation

   C. participation   D. interpretation

9. If you encounter any problem when you use this product, feel free to _____ our customer service staff.

   A. recall   B. consult

   C. instruct   D. persuade

10. My sister speaks Japanese very well, so I can _____ her when we travel to Japan.

    A. run into   B. count on

    C. look after   D. get along with

第二部分：段落填空

共 10 題，包括二個段落，每個段落各含 5 個空格。請由試題冊上四個選項中選出最適合題意的字或詞作答。

Questions 11-15

　　On August 8, 2022, a heavy rainfall ___(11)___ Seoul, the capital city of South Korea, breaking the record of the past 80 years. It caused flooding in many areas and ___(12)___ unimaginable destruction. Because of the flood, ___(13)___ . Many roads and subway stations were under water, making it impossible to commute. ___(14)___ , there was a family that died when their semi-basement home was flooded. An employee in Korea Meteorological Administration said, "It's hard not to consider the possibility that climate change causes this kind of drastic rainfall, which seems to be much more frequent than before." To prevent more casualties and help the flooded areas recover as soon as possible, the government stated that they will put all efforts on disaster relief, and provide temporary ___(15)___ and relief supplies to the victims.

11.　A.　struck
　　　B.　aroused
　　　C.　dominated
　　　D.　stimulated

12.　A.　called for
　　　B.　resulted in
　　　C.　sought after
　　　D.　fell prey to

13.　A.　gasoline prices were falling
　　　B.　the traffic was disrupted
　　　C.　it kept raining for a whole day
　　　D.　people took the subway
　　　　　instead

14.　A.　However
　　　B.　Moreover
　　　C.　Therefore
　　　D.　Nevertheless

15.　A.　addresses
　　　B.　advantages
　　　C.　acquaintances
　　　D.　accommodations

Questions 16-20

"I've never thought what is written in history books is happening in this modern society..." a victim under Russia-Ukraine war said in an interview. Since the beginning of 2022, Ukrainians have been forced to __(16)__ the brutal destruction caused by the war. Not only did the war leave Ukraine in ruins, its impact also __(17)__. The halt of export from Russia and Ukraine, which are rich in natural gas, grain, and fertilizer, made the global __(18)__ of food and fuel even worse, resulting in serious inflation around the world, especially in countries that heavily __(19)__ imported goods. __(20)__, central banks raised their interest rates in an effort to fight inflation, but consumer prices remained high.

16. A. refuse
    B. exploit
    C. witness
    D. liberate

17. A. became visible in Russia
    B. made the country unstable
    C. weakened as time went by
    D. spread through the whole world

18. A. usage
    B. shortage
    C. percentage
    D. disadvantage

19. A. rely on
    B. abide by
    C. look into
    D. deal with

20. A. However
    B. Hopefully
    C. Fortunately
    D. Accordingly

第三部分：閱讀理解

共 15 題，包括數篇短文，每篇短文後有 2~4 個相關問題。請由試題冊上四個選項中選出最適合者作答。

Questions 21-22

Train System Operation Regulations

12. Refunds under emergency situations

If the train system is out of service due to natural disasters or other emergency situations, passengers can get compensations without incurring additional charges. Those who hold single tickets, return tickets or group tickets should visit any station within two weeks to ask for a refund. For those holding periodic tickets, the expiration dates will be automatically extended. If you find the expiration date of your periodic ticket is not updated, please call our customer service.

---

21. In what situation can a passenger get a refund without paying extra fees?
   A. When the service is suspended
   B. When the service is not satisfactory
   C. When the passenger is in emergency
   D. When the passenger has a periodic ticket

22. Which of the following is **NOT** true for periodic ticket holders?
   A. They are treated differently from other passengers.
   B. They do not have to apply for compensations in person.
   C. They will automatically get their money back.
   D. They can call the customer service when needed.

第1回
第2回
第3回
第4回
第5回
第6回
第7回
第8回
第9回
第10回

Horse

Horses are four-legged animals that have long been used for transportation. Having long legs, lean body, and strong muscles, they are born to be fast runners. They are also characterized by their long head and big teeth. They prefer to live in groups, and they build strong social relationship with each other.

As familiar as they are to us, there are some facts about horses that may surprise us. For instance, horses have a range of vision of nearly 360 degrees, thanks to their eyes that are positioned on the sides of their head. However, they cannot see things right behind their head or below their nose. Fortunately, they have good sense of smell, which makes it easy for them to tell what is under their head even without seeing it.

23. Where can we most likely see this article?
    A. In a travel guide
    B. In a book review
    C. In a biology textbook
    D. In a sports magazine

24. According to the article, what helps horses run fast?
    A. Slim figure
    B. Long head
    C. Wide vision
    D. Preference for living together

25. About horses' vision, which of the following is true?
    A. They can see everything around them.
    B. They cannot see things ahead of them.
    C. The positions of their eyes contribute to their wide vision.
    D. They rely more on their sense of smell than their sight.

第1回
第2回
第3回
第4回
第5回
第6回
第7回
第8回
第9回
第10回

Questions 26-28 are based on information provided in the following article and email.

SnowChat Introduces New Parental Control Feature

Parental control feature has been added to the latest release of the SnowChat app, the fastest-growing social media app last year. According to a latest survey, up to 71% of teenagers are using SnowChat, which is available for those who are 13 years of age or older.

In addition to text messaging, users can share photos and short clips on SnowChat. Due to the lack of monitoring, nude and violent content can easily be seen on the platform. Since the majority of its users are teenagers, the platform is faced with the responsibility to control the distribution of such content and let parents know how their children interact with others online.

Therefore, SnowChat introduced the new feature especially for those worried parents. Parents of children aged 13-18 can now see which accounts their children are messaging with, and if they find an account sending inappropriate content, they can report to SnowChat. SnowChat states that it hopes to ensure a healthy environment for young people to have fun without being exposed to harmful content.

From:	Penny.wang@qmail.com
To:	service@snowchat.com
Subject:	Please help!

To whom it may concern,

I appreciate that you introduced the feature for parents to see how their children use your app. However, I found there is a flaw in the feature. Children can easily get around its control by registering with a false birth date. At my son's age, he can use your app, but he is supposed to be monitored with the new feature. Yet he pretended to be 20 while registering, making it impossible for me to check his activities. Please let me know how to fix the problem.

Regards,
Penny Wang

第 1 回

第 2 回

26. What is the main purpose of the article?
    A. To stress the importance of forbidding inappropriate content
    B. To reveal how many teenagers are using SnowChat
    C. To introduce a new feature of SnowChat
    D. To promote a new social media app

第 3 回

第 4 回

27. Based on the article, which of the following is true?
    A. SnowChat is not popular with teenagers.
    B. Users cannot upload videos on SnowChat.
    C. Children younger than 13 cannot use SnowChat.
    D. Parents can directly ban accounts with the SnowChat's new feature.

第 5 回

第 6 回

28. What can we infer about Ms. Wang?
    A. Her son is under 18.
    B. She lied to the app about her age.
    C. She thinks the new feature is practical.
    D. She has an open mind about her son's activities online.

第 7 回

第 8 回

第 9 回

第 10 回

The idea of remote learning has been around for many years, but it was the COVID-19 pandemic that made it a norm. As a measure to implement social distancing and slow down the spread of the virus, schools shut down and provided online classes instead.

Many students find it less stressful to learn from the comfort of their homes, while some feel unhappy when they do so. Due to the lack of in-person interaction with classmates and teachers, students may feel isolated and have lower motivation to be engaged in class. Such effects can increase the risk of depression among students.

Remote learning also proved to be less effective in general. Students find it hard to focus on their computer screens, and thus learn less as a result. Such a situation is especially negative for those in their last year of high school, as they may end up academically unprepared for college and have difficulty catching up.

To deal with this problem, colleges have built summer programs aiming to bridge students into higher education. These programs saved many "victims" of the pandemic, as they can strengthen their skills on subjects they have not learned well online.

29. What is the main purpose of this article?
    A. To look back at the pandemic years
    B. To propose a new method of learning
    C. To discuss the disadvantages of remote learning
    D. To raise awareness about learning disabilities

30. According to the article, what is true about remote learning?
    A. It was invented during the pandemic.
    B. It has to be achieved through social distancing.
    C. It is an alternative to in-person learning.
    D. It improves students' academic performance.

31. Which of the following is **NOT** mentioned as what students are faced with when learning online?
    A. Worse learning outcomes
    B. Difficulty graduating
    C. Reluctance to learn
    D. Mental issues

32. Who does the word "victims" in the last paragraph refer to?
    A. COVID-19 patients
    B. High school dropouts
    C. Academically struggling students
    D. Students experiencing depression

第1回
第2回
第3回
第4回
第5回
第6回
第7回
第8回
第9回
第10回

As more and more people become conscious of the impact of their food choices on the environment and animal welfare, vegetarianism and veganism are gaining popularity. Both kinds of diets avoid meat, fish, and seafood, yet vegetarians can consume some animal products, such as eggs and dairy products. Vegans, on the other hand, try their best to avoid all kinds of animal products. There are also some people who choose plant-based diet because of their religious beliefs, which have different restrictions on food choices.

No matter why a person chooses to go vegetarian or vegan, they should have a well-balanced diet plan with special focus on the intake of protein, which is harder to obtain from fruits and vegetables. Those who need special attention to their nutrition, such as pregnant women and children, should be especially careful before eliminating meat from their diet.

Despite the risk of malnutrition, plant-based diet can be beneficial to health as long as they are well-planned and provide necessary nutrients. Multiple studies show that health issues such as overweight, diabetes, and heart diseases are less prevalent among those who do not eat meat. With more researchers working on this topic, we can expect to see more benefits of plant-based diet in the future.

33. Which is the best title for this article?
   A. How Meatless Diets Became Mainstream
   B. To Go Vegetarian or Go Vegan, That is the Question
   C. Meat-Free Diet: Balancing the Risks and Benefits
   D. Plant-Based Diet: The Ultimate Health Solution

34. What is the difference between vegetarians and vegans?
   A. Vegetarians eat eggs daily.
   B. Vegetarians can eat meat once in a while.
   C. Vegans have more restrictions on their diet.
   D. Vegans are more likely to have religious beliefs.

35. Based on the article, which of the following is true?
   A. Those who do not eat meat are more likely to have low protein intake.
   B. Plant-based diets are especially beneficial to pregnant women and children.
   C. Patients of diabetes and heart diseases can cure themselves by not eating meat.
   D. Only a few researchers are interested in the benefits of meat-free diets.

第1回
第2回
第3回
第4回
第5回
第6回
第7回
第8回
第9回
第10回

TEST 03

GEPT 全民英檢

中級初試

題目本

本測驗分四部分，全為四選一之選擇題，共 35 題，作答時間約 30 分鐘。

第一部分：看圖辨義

共 5 題，試題冊上有數幅圖畫，每一圖畫有 1~3 個描述該圖的題目，每題請聽光碟放音機播出題目以及四個英語敘述之後，選出與所看到的圖畫最相符的答案，每題只播出一遍。

例：（看）

（聽）

Look at the picture. What is the woman doing?

A. She is looking at a sculpture.

B. She is appreciating a painting.

C. She is picking up a handbag.

D. She is entering a museum.

正確答案為 B。

聽力測驗第一部分自本頁開始。

A. Question 1

 # Class Schedule

	Monday	Tuesday	Wednesday	Thursday	Friday
8-10	Math	Science	English	Social Studies	History
10-12	P.E.	Music	Art	Geography	Computer

Lunch Time

第1回
第2回
第3回
第4回
第5回
第6回
第7回
第8回
第9回
第10回

B. Questions 2 and 3

5-DAY FORECAST

DAY	Mon.	Tue.	Wed.	Thu.	Fri.
WEATHER	☂	☂	⛅	⛅	☀
CHANCE OF RAIN	80%	70%	40%	30%	10%
MAX TEMP.	15°C	20°C	15°C	25°C	30°C
MIN TEMP.	11°C	14°C	11°C	20°C	27°C

C. Questions 4 and 5

Opening Party

Wendy's Glam Studio

Welcome
Saturday, October 15
3:00 PM
13 Rolly Avenue, Panorama City

Free Entry | Free Parking | Food and Music

Services: Hair Styling, Skin Care, Body Waxing, Nail Care   Phone: 2222-2828
Open MON-SAT, 9AM-5PM

第二部分：問答

共 10 題，每題請聽光碟放音機播出一英語問句或直述句之後，從試題冊上 A、B、C、D 四個回答或回應中，選出一個最適合者作答。每題只播出一遍。

例：（聽）Now that we've come to Kenting, we should try water sports.
　　（看）A. You can try harder next time.
　　　　　B. Yes. I'm on the way there.
　　　　　C. That sounds exciting to me.
　　　　　D. We are coming in an hour.

正確答案為 C。

6. A. I've been driving since I was 20.
　　B. It won't be long until the bus arrives.
　　C. About 30 minutes by car.
　　D. You'll see your destination on the right.

7. A. The party was a hit.
　　B. I didn't see it coming.
　　C. It made me exhausted.
　　D. I felt excited going there.

8. A. Well, I think that's a good sign.
　　B. The contract number has been changed.
　　C. Yes, its design is really excellent.
　　D. No, he still needs time to review it.

9. A. I agree. It's made of finest cotton.
　　B. No, I haven't paid for it.
　　C. Maybe we need to check other bed frames.
　　D. Yeah, it's not too firm or too soft.

10. A. He has booked another venue.
　　B. He has a scheduling conflict.
　　C. We have achieved the goal.
　　D. We want to make it more productive.

第1回
第2回
第3回
第4回
第5回
第6回
第7回
第8回
第9回
第10回

11. A. Yes, I will visit one of my friends.
     B. The train will come in thirty minutes.
     C. Go straight and turn left at the corner.
     D. You can buy the tickets there.

12. A. I read books in my leisure time.
     B. I can donate them to a charity.
     C. I can finish it in an hour.
     D. The old books are on sale.

13. A. She failed to catch the plane.
     B. The flight number should be corrected.
     C. I can pick her up if you're busy.
     D. I want to delay our flight.

14. A. She is not available tomorrow night.
     B. I believe she will handle it well.
     C. We need some help with the project.
     D. She didn't reply to my message.

15. A. The manager will hold a party.
     B. The department store isn't open yet.
     C. It will hire some new employees.
     D. Mr. Johnson has a great chance.

第三部分：簡短對話

共 10 題，每題請聽光碟放音機播出一段對話及一個相關的問題後，從試題冊上 A、B、C、D 四個選項中選出一個最適合者作答。每段對話及問題只播出一遍。

例：（聽）（Woman） Excuse me. Does the next train go to the airport?

（Man） No. Actually, this is the high speed rail station. You should go to the airport MRT station nearby to get to the airport.

（Woman） Thank you for letting me know. This is my first time taking a train to the airport, so I didn't notice that.

Question: What happened to the woman?

（看）A. She missed her train.
B. She got on the wrong train.
C. She went to the wrong station.
D. Her flight has already left.

正確答案為 C。

16. A. Planning for their summer vacation.
    B. Talking about a tourist spot.
    C. Searching for some information.
    D. Exploring a gorgeous island.

17. A. Its prices are reasonable.
    B. The waiters served very well.
    C. It didn't meet his expectations.
    D. He went there to celebrate his birthday.

18. A. He still has work to do.
    B. He does not trust the doctor.
    C. He has a date with his co-workers.
    D. He is on a business trip.

19. A. The reason for a breakup.
    B. The meaning of a saying.
    C. The types of music they like.
    D. Psychological effect of music.

20. A. Find out the location of the concert.
    B. See if there are tickets available.
    C. Learn about when ticket sale begins.
    D. Pay for the tickets he has ordered.

第 1 回
第 2 回
第 3 回
第 4 回
第 5 回
第 6 回
第 7 回
第 8 回
第 9 回
第 10 回

21. A. Pressure from her work.
    B. Lack of sleep.
    C. Physical health issues.
    D. Bad performance at work.

22. A. Bring the letter to Ms. Andrews.
    B. Send the letter to the right address.
    C. Return the letter to the post office.
    D. Open the envelope to read the letter.

23. A. He is late for a meeting.
    B. He got lost on the way.
    C. His car needs to be repaired.
    D. He has missed his train.

24.

Sapphire Gym Yearly Membership Plans			
	Basic Equipment	Swimming Pool	Personal Training Classes
Standard $300	●	✕	✕
Silver $500	●	✕	5
Gold $800	●	●	5
Platinum $1000	●	●	10

    A. Standard.
    B. Silver.
    C. Gold.
    D. Platinum.

25. **Salesperson Training Sessions**

Date	Topic	Speaker
Thu., July 28	Presentation skills	David Thompson
Tue., August 9	Customer relations	Ellie Hamilton
Fri., August 19	Selling skills	Ben Johnson
Wed., August 24	Time management	Jim Walter

    A. David Thompson.
    B. Ellie Hamilton.
    C. Ben Johnson.
    D. Jim Walter.

第四部分：簡短談話

共 10 題，每題請聽光碟放音機播出一段談話及一個相關的問題後，從試題冊上 A、B、C、D 四個選項中選出一個最適合者作答。每段談話及問題只播出一遍。

例： （聽）Teenagers can easily feel hurt in their social lives. When they have difficulty making friends, they may feel worried about going to school. Even if they are popular at school, they may be persuaded to do things they don't like, such as smoking or drinking, under peer pressure. The stress of fitting in can eventually make them mentally ill.

Question: According to the speaker, what makes a teenager try smoking even though they are not interested?

（看） A. Parents' complaint.
B. Friends' persuasion.
C. Romantic relationship.
D. Academic pressure.

正確答案為 B。

26. A. It is on discount.
    B. It has a bigger screen.
    C. Its battery life is long.
    D. It is not available online.

27. A. Responding to Diana's request.
    B. Saying farewell to Diana.
    C. Giving a presentation to Diana.
    D. Giving feedback on Diana's work.

28. A. The evolution of hairdryers.
    B. The popularity of hairdryers.
    C. The first hairdryer in the world.
    D. The functions of hairdryers.

29. A. The activities to be prepared.
    B. Things to bring to the picnic.
    C. Whether Nancy is interested.
    D. Whether Nancy will have free time.

30. A. To promote in-theater food service.
    B. To prevent littering in the cinema.
    C. To ensure a pleasant viewing experience.
    D. To prepare for a talk after the movie.

31. A. It was done efficiently.
    B. It was done with some friends' help.
    C. It was interrupted by something else.
    D. It was forgotten and not started at all.

32. A. They all volunteer on their own will.
    B. They volunteer after graduating.
    C. They get good grades in academic subjects.
    D. They get the chance to learn outside class.

33. A. Broadcast a message.
    B. Confirm his mother's name.
    C. Take him to the central square.
    D. Send people to find his mother.

34.

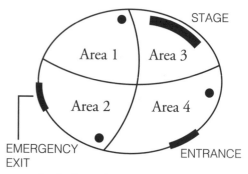

A. In Area 1.
B. In Area 2.
C. In Area 3.
D. In Area 4.

35.

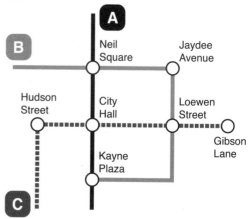

A. Neil Square.
B. City Hall.
C. Loewen Street.
D. Kayne Plaza.

本測驗分三部分，全為四選一之選擇題，共 35 題，作答時間 45 分鐘。

第一部分：詞彙

共 10 題，每題含一個空格。請由試題冊上的四個選項中選出最適合題意的字或詞作答。

1. The famous museum _____ historic objects of ancient Egypt.
   - A. features
   - B. supports
   - C. attracts
   - D. encloses

2. Even though James _____ a lot of challenges, he worked hard to overcome them and achieved success.
   - A. heard of
   - B. came up with
   - C. was faced with
   - D. took advantage of

3. The _____ provides a list of required ingredients for making pancakes, along with detailed instructions on the steps of the process.
   - A. receipt
   - B. recipe
   - C. catalog
   - D. agenda

4. Proper nutrition and regular exercise are _____ to maintaining physical health.
   - A. luxurious
   - B. fundamental
   - C. literary
   - D. insignificant

5. Having worked all day without eating anything, Sabrina is _____ now.
   - A. charming
   - B. cherishing
   - C. starving
   - D. stitching

6. Some influencers have mental health problems due to the negative _____ they receive on social media.
   - A. comments
   - B. commissions
   - C. consultants
   - D. connections

7. Jerry's interest in fashion design _____ his childhood experience of watching his mother sewing clothes for him.
   A. relies on
   B. stems from
   C. gives in to
   D. puts up with

8. Even the most experienced doctors cannot _____ of the success of every surgery, as there are always risks involved.
   A. assure
   B. approve
   C. be accused
   D. be composed

9. After a heated discussion, the jury finally reached the _____ that the man was innocent.
   A. objective
   B. achievement
   C. status
   D. conclusion

10. Taking notes is an effective _____ for students to remember what is taught in class.
    A. tragedy
    B. strategy
    C. penalty
    D. modesty

第二部分：段落填空

共 10 題，包括二個段落，每個段落各含 5 個空格。請由試題冊上四個選項中選出最適合題意的字或詞作答。

Questions 11-15

Australia is a popular tourist destination for those seeking the beauty of nature. __(11)__, however, it becomes challenging to maintain its popularity and primitive charm at the same time. For instance, the Great Barrier Reef attracts many visitors to __(12)__ its stunning coral formations and diverse marine life, but they may also pollute or break off parts of the reef, causing stress to the corals. Although there are __(13)__ on responsible tourism, which most people try to follow, it is still inevitable that some will harm the environment, either accidentally or __(14)__. Therefore, it is important for the __(15)__ to take steps to minimize the impact of tourism on the environment, such as enforcing stricter laws and promoting eco-tourism. By doing so, it is possible that we preserve the environment while allowing tourists to enjoy nature.

11. A. Due to its declining popularity these years
    B. As the number of tourists increases
    C. Because of its distance from other continents
    D. When it comes to the benefits of tourism

12. A. appreciate
    B. encounter
    C. interpret
    D. suspect

13. A. feedbacks
    B. guidelines
    C. implications
    D. circumstances

14. A. in vain
    B. at ease
    C. on purpose
    D. without fail

15. A. department
    B. organization
    C. management
    D. administration

第 1 回
第 2 回
第 3 回
第 4 回
第 5 回
第 6 回
第 7 回
第 8 回
第 9 回
第 10 回

Questions 16-20

Twins can be classified into two types: identical and non-identical. The difference is whether the twins ___(16)___ the same fertilized(受精的) egg. Identical twins, who are formed when a single fertilized egg divide into separate embryos (胚胎), usually have very similar ___(17)___. On the contrary, non-identical twins are the result of two or more fertilized eggs, and therefore look different.

___(18)___, it is usually identical twins that come to our mind because their nearly identical look captures our attention and imagination. There are many novels and movies, especially mysterious ones, that ___(19)___ identical twins. The fact that identical twins look very similar can create confusion in the story and lead to unexpected plot twists when they pretend to be each other or reveal their identity. Also, they are often ___(20)___ as having a special or even supernatural connection, adding to the sense of mystery that surrounds them.

16. A. carry out
    B. develop from
    C. account for
    D. look up

17. A. evidence
    B. appearance
    C. motivation
    D. recreation

18. A. Considering the studies
    B. Since twins are so special
    C. In spite of their obvious
       difference
    D. When we talk about twins

19. A. apply to
    B. depend on
    C. run through
    D. center around

20. A. displayed
    B. portrayed
    C. exhibited
    D. submitted

第三部分：閱讀理解

共 15 題，包括數篇短文，每篇短文後有 2~4 個相關問題。請由試題冊上四個選項中選出最適合者作答。

Questions 21-22

Potter's Gardening

If you are interested in gardening but do not know how to start, Potter's Gardening is here to help. Our staff can provide you with valuable advice and guidance on how to start your garden, choose the right plants for your space, and maintain your garden. In addition to consultation, we also provide services such as watering, weeding, and lawn mowing, which save you time and trouble. Contact us today to learn about how we can help you plant a beautiful and healthy garden.

Special Offer
For the first 100 customers only!
Free consultation and 15% off on all other services

Phone: 2222-8888   Email: pottergarden@premail.com

---

21. What is true about Potter's Gardening?
    A. People can buy some plants there.
    B. It offers courses on gardening.
    C. Its staff will visit its clients' gardens and give advice.
    D. It can help reduce the hassle of gardening.

22. What is true about Potter's Gardening's special offer?
    A. It is provided on a regular basis.
    B. People must make a phone call to enjoy the offer.
    C. Its consultation service is now 15% off.
    D. Lawn mowing service is currently offered at a discount.

Harrisburg Furniture Incorporation

145 Weldon Parkway, Phoenix, AZ

November 21
Mr. Meyer Caldwell
809 Village Central Avenue, Tucson, AZ

Dear Mr. Caldwell,

I am writing to inform you about the order you have placed with Harrisburg Furniture. Unfortunately, due to the shortage of maple wood, the cabinet you have ordered is still unavailable, and it will not be restocked until mid-February.

You can wait until the cabinet becomes available again, or you can consider the same model made of other kinds of wood, such as oak and walnut (胡桃). If you choose to change the material, your cabinet will be ready in three weeks. As a gesture of apology, we will offer you a discount of 20%, no matter you decide on a different material or not. If you want to know more about the characteristics and properties of each kind of wood, you are welcome to stop by our store and consult our staff.

Thank you for your understanding in this matter. Please accept our sincere apology again for any inconvenience this may have caused. If you have any further questions or concerns, please do not hesitate to contact us.

Sincerely,
Leanne McMichael
Manager, Harrisburg Furniture

23. What is the main purpose of this letter?
    A. To introduce the latest promotions
    B. To report a problem with an order
    C. To recommend canceling an order
    D. To express that other kinds of wood are better

24. According to the letter, why is the product not available?
    A. There is currently a lack of material.
    B. It is very popular among customers.
    C. It will not be manufactured anymore.
    D. The manufacturer is closed until February.

25. What does Ms. McMichael suggest about the problem?
    A. The order can be fulfilled earlier if the material is changed.
    B. Mr. Caldwell can get a discount by changing his order.
    C. Mr. Caldwell cannot but choose a different model of cabinet.
    D. To change the order, it is necessary to visit the store.

第 1 回
第 2 回
第 3 回
第 4 回
第 5 回
第 6 回
第 7 回
第 8 回
第 9 回
第 10 回

Time to Renew your Membership!

Thank you so much for your dedication to Franklin Country Club. Without your loyalty and support, we would not be able to continuously provide our members with valuable benefits. In the next year, we have bigger plans, such as upgrading some of the facilities in our club. However, we need your help to make it happen!

As a token of our appreciation, we are pleased to offer the following benefits to our members in the next whole year:

- a special birthday gift from Spencer Boutique
- a voucher booklet worth over $500
- 20% discount on food & drinks
- Free access for the member and one accompanying non-member to our facilities (additional non-members will be charged regular fees)

You can visit our website (franklincountryclub.com) for more details. We hope that you take advantage of these benefits and continue to enjoy all that Franklin Country Club has to offer.

From:	JoeChapman@geemail.com
To:	service@franklincountryclub.com
Subject:	Question about membership

Dear Sir/Madam,

I am already a member, and I am considering to obtain membership for my family, too. My two children recently started learning to play tennis, and I am interested in having them use the club's tennis court to practice and improve their skills. My wife and I would also like to watch them play and support them in their development. Should I make them all members, or are there better deals for our case?

Thank you for your time, and I look forward to hearing back from you soon.

Regards,
Joe Chapman

26. What is implied about Franklin Country Club?
    A. It has recently renewed its facilities.
    B. Its membership fee is $500.
    C. Its membership is renewed every year.
    D. Only members can use its facilities.

27. Which of the following is **NOT** a benefit for the members of Franklin Country Club?
    A. A birthday gift made by the club
    B. Special coupons
    C. Buying food at lower prices
    D. Free access to its facilities

28. How many more people in Mr. Chapman's family should become a member to avoid being charged regular fee for using the tennis court of Franklin Country Club?
    A. 0
    B. 1
    C. 2
    D. 3

Questions 29-31

    In the annual National Youth Tobacco Survey of 2022, 14% of high school students said that they are e-cigarette users. Among those who use e-cigarettes, half of them "vape" (i.e. use e-cigarettes) 20 to 30 days a month, and one-fourth of them vape every day. The same survey last year showed that 11% of high school students were using e-cigarettes, but due to the different situations in which the two surveys were conducted, it is not appropriate to jump to the conclusion that the young population using e-cigarettes is growing quickly. The survey of 2021 was conducted when many schools were closed due to the pandemic, while the survey of 2022 was conducted when schools were mostly open.

    Regardless of whether there are actually more young people using e-cigarettes, it is a fact that e-cigarettes have become more popular than traditional cigarettes among high school students. Some of them are attracted by the various flavors of e-cigarettes, and they are under the impression that e-cigarettes are less harmful to health than traditional ones. Despite that research has shown that e-cigarettes can cause equal amounts of health risks, e-cigarette vendors still try to mislead the public with slogans such as "e-cigarettes can help quit smoking", "e-cigarettes are harmless" and "e-cigarettes are not cigarettes", which can contribute to young people's incorrect knowledge about the risks of using e-cigarettes.

29. What is this article mainly about?
    A. The current situation of the e-cigarette industry
    B. The correct method to conduct a survey
    C. Health risks of smoking e-cigarettes
    D. The use of e-cigarettes among teenagers

30. Why cannot the surveys in 2021 and 2022 be directly compared?
    A. They were conducted using different methods.
    B. There were not enough samples in the survey in 2021.
    C. They are conducted by different organizations.
    D. The results of the survey in 2021 might be affected by the pandemic.

31. What does the second paragraph suggest can be a reason that teenagers are attracted by e-cigarettes?
    A. The fact that some of their peers are using e-cigarettes
    B. Wrong information spread by some enterprises
    C. The desire to rebel against authority and regulations
    D. The cool image that is associated with e-cigarettes

第1回
第2回
第3回
第4回
第5回
第6回
第7回
第8回
第9回
第10回

LOHAS, an abbreviation(縮寫) for Lifestyles of Health and Sustainability(永續性), refers to the consumer movement interested in healthy living as well as social and environmental issues. As more and more people embrace the idea of LOHAS, organic, natural, and eco-friendly products see significant growth in demand. For example, products made from recycled materials have become more popular among those who are conscious about reducing waste and preserving the environment.

Long before the term "LOHAS" was invented, however, a company called "Freitag" already started making bags from recycled materials, such as seatbelts and airbags of retired cars, and even construction site waste. For used bags, it also provides repair and recycle services. Recently, it started making phone cases made from ski boots, and its ultimate goal is to turn everything that is typically considered waste into useful objects. Furthermore, it also demonstrated its commitment to sustainability by constructing its flagship store(旗艦店) in Zurich with used shipping containers.

While companies play an important role in promoting LOHAS through their products and practices, it is also up to individuals to embrace this lifestyle and make sustainable choices. For example, instead of buying products with beautiful but too much packaging, consumers may consider products that do not have an inviting look but are more environmentally friendly. They may also want to pay extra for sustainable products to support environmentally responsible practices. It may seem inconvenient or costly to make such choices, but it can benefit the planet and create a better future for generations to come.

32. What is this article mainly about?
    A. The history and significance of LOHAS
    B. Various methods of living a LOHAS lifestyle
    C. How a company can succeed by practicing LOHAS
    D. The relation between consumer market and LOHAS

33. Which of the following can best describe Freitag?
    A. A waste recycling company
    B. A select shop based in Zurich
    C. A company making sustainable products
    D. An environmentally conscious service provider

34. Which of the following is true about Freitag?
    A. It was established because of the LOHAS trend.
    B. It helps its customers to restore the products they have bought.
    C. Its product line is limited to bags only.
    D. Its flagship store in Zurich carries various kinds of containers.

35. What can be inferred from the article?
    A. LOHAS is more like a marketing strategy than a real consumer trend.
    B. People should avoid buying beautiful products to be environmentally responsible.
    C. Sustainable products are more competitive in their prices.
    D. Consumers should balance their choices to practice LOHAS.

第 1 回
第 2 回
第 3 回
第 4 回
第 5 回
第 6 回
第 7 回
第 8 回
第 9 回
第 10 回

TEST 04

GEPT
全民英檢
中級初試

題目本

本測驗分四部分，全為四選一之選擇題，共 35 題，作答時間約 30 分鐘。

第一部分：看圖辨義

共 5 題，試題冊上有數幅圖畫，每一圖畫有 1~3 個描述該圖的題目，每題請聽光碟放音機播出題目以及四個英語敘述之後，選出與所看到的圖畫最相符的答案，每題只播出一遍。

例：（看）

（聽）

Look at the picture. What is the woman doing?

A. She is looking at a sculpture.

B. She is appreciating a painting.

C. She is picking up a handbag.

D. She is entering a museum.

正確答案為 B。

聽力測驗第一部分自本頁開始。

A. Question 1

第1回
第2回
第3回
第4回
第5回
第6回
第7回
第8回
第9回
第10回

B. Questions 2 and 3

Harvest Moon Festival

Date	Time	Performer	Place
Sep. 8	20:00	Choppers Folk Guitar Club	Fossil Ocean
Sep. 15	19:30	Funky Fiona Jazz Band	City Park
Sep. 22	15:00	Greenery High School Chorus	City Park
Sep. 29	20:30	Marvin String Orchestra	Stella Plaza

● In case of rainy days, please check our website for updated dates.

C. Questions 4 and 5

Jimmy's Kitchen

Food		Drink	
Hamburger	$4.99	Apple Juice	$2.79
French Fries	$1.79	Coke	$1.49
Hot Dog	$3.99	Milkshake	$2.49
Apple Pie	$1.99	Lemon Black Tea	$1.99

第二部分：問答

共 10 題，每題請聽光碟放音機播出一英語問句或直述句之後，從試題冊上 A、B、C、D 四個回答或回應中，選出一個最適合者作答。每題只播出一遍。

例：（聽）Now that we've come to Kenting, we should try water sports.

（看）A. You can try harder next time.

B. Yes. I'm on the way there.

C. That sounds exciting to me.

D. We are coming in an hour.

正確答案為 C。

6. A. Yes, my parents will come next week.
   B. Then we need to prepare some food.
   C. No, I didn't watch the weather forecast.
   D. I think I'm good. Thanks anyway.

7. A. I prefer desserts over salty snacks.
   B. I didn't see anything at the corner.
   C. Let's grab a bite next time.
   D. Great! I love shopping for groceries.

8. A. I'm scared of watching horror films.
   B. I just went to the bookstore yesterday.
   C. Do you know dragons are fictional?
   D. Can I borrow it after you finish reading?

9. A. Sara needs a pair of shoes.
   B. The supermarket is open every weekday.
   C. I think we're running out of milk.
   D. Yes, we sell many kinds of vegetables.

10. A. Turn left and you'll see it.
    B. Remember to take medicine on time.
    C. No pharmacist is on duty now.
    D. I've been there once.

第 1 回
第 2 回
第 3 回
第 4 回
第 5 回
第 6 回
第 7 回
第 8 回
第 9 回
第 10 回

11. A. Do they live in Southern Taiwan?
    B. Oh, are they doing well?
    C. How are your parents recently?
    D. I think we need to go on a trip!

12. A. I am really bad at dancing.
    B. I play table tennis once in a while.
    C. He's not good at running.
    D. I've been jogging for two hours.

13. A. I don't think I should pick it up.
    B. You can come at your convenience.
    C. Which 7-Eleven do you mean?
    D. Sure, where should I go then?

14. A. We already did it last year.
    B. No, the final score is 7 to 9.
    C. I've heard it is next week.
    D. The pop-up quiz was so hard!

15. A. Have you asked your advisor for help?
    B. I've done some research about science.
    C. I thought the manager approved the project.
    D. I definitely need more time on this.

第三部分：簡短對話

第1回
第2回
第3回
第4回
第5回
第6回
第7回
第8回
第9回
第10回

共 10 題，每題請聽光碟放音機播出一段對話及一個相關的問題後，從試題冊上 A、B、C、D 四個選項中選出一個最適合者作答。每段對話及問題只播出一遍。

例：（聽）（Woman） Excuse me. Does the next train go to the airport?

（Man） No. Actually, this is the high speed rail station. You should go to the airport MRT station nearby to get to the airport.

（Woman） Thank you for letting me know. This is my first time taking a train to the airport, so I didn't notice that.

Question: What happened to the woman?

（看）A. She missed her train.

B. She got on the wrong train.

C. She went to the wrong station.

D. Her flight has already left.

正確答案為 C。

16. A. Work in her office.
    B. Work from her home.
    C. Go to the concert alone.
    D. Go to the concert with the man.

17. A. Purchase a piece of furniture.
    B. Bring the receipt to the store.
    C. Search for a missing item.
    D. Get a refund.

18. A. A farewell party.
    B. A bachelor party.
    C. A retirement party.
    D. A birthday party.

19. A. Booking a hotel room.
    B. Reserving a table at a restaurant.
    C. Booking a flight.
    D. Buying a train ticket.

20. A. At an animal shelter.
    B. At the city hall.
    C. At a volunteer's home.
    D. On the street.

21. A. Go to the supermarket.
    B. Clear the yard.
    C. Fix the broken window.
    D. Check the weather forecast.

22.   A. The woman will not teach him.
      B. The woman will make fun of
         him.
      C. The video game is expensive.
      D. They may have a fight.

23.   A. Preparing to play a sport.
      B. Competing in the Olympics.
      C. Playing badminton.
      D. Watching an Olympic game.

24.

50cm

$99.9

35cm

$29.9

25cm

$50→$40

15cm

$35→$25

      A. The mirror.
      B. The vase.
      C. The teddy bear.
      D. The candle holder.

25.

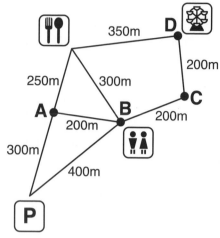

      A. At location A.
      B. At location B.
      C. At location C.
      D. At location D.

第四部分：簡短談話

共 10 題，每題請聽光碟放音機播出一段談話及一個相關的問題後，從試題冊上 A、B、C、D 四個選項中選出一個最適合者作答。每段談話及問題只播出一遍。

例：（聽）Teenagers can easily feel hurt in their social lives. When they have difficulty making friends, they may feel worried about going to school. Even if they are popular at school, they may be persuaded to do things they don't like, such as smoking or drinking, under peer pressure. The stress of fitting in can eventually make them mentally ill.

Question: According to the speaker, what makes a teenager try smoking even though they are not interested?

（看）A. Parents' complaint.
B. Friends' persuasion.
C. Romantic relationship.
D. Academic pressure.

正確答案為 B。

26. A. To look for a kid.
B. To help a boy find his parents.
C. To promote some children's clothes.
D. To promote child safety.

27. A. A construction company.
B. Her colleague.
C. Her landlord.
D. Her tenant.

28. A. High speed.
B. Large storage capacity.
C. Light weight.
D. Great battery life.

29. A. His education background.
B. His job experience.
C. His achievements.
D. His attitude.

30. A. The catchy song.
B. The hurricane.
C. High temperature.
D. Windy weather.

31. A. Garbage trucks will not come.
    B. Garbage trucks will come earlier.
    C. Garbage will be dumped on City Square.
    D. Recyclable waste will not be accepted.

32. A. Some treasure.
    B. Some stationery.
    C. A board game.
    D. Free admission.

33. A. Designing the building.
    B. Raising fund for the building.
    C. Giving a speech.
    D. Leading the company.

34.

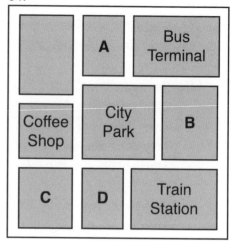

    A. Location A.
    B. Location B.
    C. Location C.
    D. Location D.

35.

	Saturday	Sunday
Morning	Sally Kendal	
Afternoon		Bill Mosby
Evening	John Anderson	Marshal Bradly

    A. Sally Kendal.
    B. John Anderson.
    C. Bill Mosby.
    D. Marshal Bradly.

本測驗分三部分，全為四選一之選擇題，共 35 題，作答時間 45 分鐘。

第一部分：詞彙

共 10 題，每題含一個空格。請由試題冊上的四個選項中選出最適合題意的字或詞作答。

1. There are many kinds of _____ we can use to describe our feelings.
   A. expressions
   B. measurements
   C. conclusions
   D. agreements

2. Mr. Smith enjoys _____ sports a lot, such as bungee jumping and skydiving.
   A. extreme
   B. accurate
   C. existing
   D. outstanding

3. Our new product will be _____ in both physical stores and our online shop.
   A. frequent
   B. unique
   C. available
   D. regretful

4. During the _____ ceremony, each student goes on the stage to receive their diploma.
   A. award
   B. promotion
   C. graduation
   D. retirement

5. Those who want to register for this course should _____ this form and submit it to our staff.
   A. fill out
   B. write down
   C. sign up for
   D. take care of

6. We encourage every user to _____ the app to the latest version, which has many new features.
   A. update
   B. extend
   C. refresh
   D. download

第 1 回
第 2 回
第 3 回
第 4 回
第 5 回
第 6 回
第 7 回
第 8 回
第 9 回
第 10 回

7. The company conducts surveys regularly to understand how it can better
   _____ customers' needs.
   A. satisfy   B. qualify
   C. simplify   D. intensify

8. Since this restaurant is very popular, you need to make a reservation
   _____.
   A. by chance   B. in advance
   C. by yourself   D. in a hurry

9. The country received a huge amount of _____ after being seriously hit by
   the earthquake.
   A. tensions   B. donations
   C. suspicions   D. inspections

10. You may have a better chance of getting a job if you show more _____
    during an interview.
    A. evidence   B. existence
    C. innocence   D. confidence

第三部分：閱讀理解

共 15 題，包括數篇短文，每篇短文後有 2~4 個相關問題。請由試題冊上四個選項中選出最適合者作答。

Questions 11-15

When you walk on a beach, you may notice trash here and there. Most of the trash is ___(11)___ to the beach by wind or water. Regular beach cleanups may help, but it is more important to reduce waste at the source. Governments around the world have taken various ___(12)___ to reduce waste. In Taiwan, for example, the government ___(13)___ people to bring their own cups by offering a discount to those who do so when buying drinks. ___(14)___, there are actions against the use of disposable tableware in restaurants. ___(15)___ disposable products, we can reduce the amount of waste and help protect the environment.

11. A. blown
     B. driven
     C. thrown
     D. carried

12. A. targets
     B. policies
     C. measures
     D. perspectives

13. A. forces
     B. allows
     C. expects
     D. encourages

14. A. Likewise
     B. Namely
     C. Therefore
     D. Otherwise

15. A. By cutting the use of
     B. To stop manufacturing
     C. Considering the impact of
     D. Contrary to conventional views about

第 1 回
第 2 回
第 3 回
第 4 回
第 5 回
第 6 回
第 7 回
第 8 回
第 9 回
第 10 回

Questions 16-20

Sloths are mammals   (16)   to the rainforests of Central and South America. They are known for moving very slowly, normally at a speed of 4 meters per minute on the tree, and only 2 meters per minute on the ground.   (17) , if a sloth falls on the ground, it may be at risk of being   (18)   by jaguars (美洲豹). Sloths are not only slow-moving animals, but they also have a slow digestion process.   (19) , it takes them almost a month to digest. Despite being slow in many aspects, sloths are actually good swimmers.   (20)   their long arms, they can swim three times faster than they move on the ground.

16. A. vital
    B. loyal
    C. native
    D. related

17. A. Therefore
    B. However
    C. Nevertheless
    D. Timely

18. A. tickled
    B. hunted
    C. nurtured
    D. caressed

19. A. Once they are ready
    B. After they finish a meal
    C. Although they move slowly
    D. When they become hungry

20. A. Despite
    B. Thanks to
    C. Rather than
    D. For the sake of

第三部分：閱讀理解

共 15 題，包括數篇短文，每篇短文後有 2~4 個相關問題。請由試題冊上四個選項中選出最適合者作答。

Questions 21-22

Memorandum

September 28, 2025
From: Management office
To: All residents
Subject: Elevator maintenance

Elevators no. 1 and 3 are going to be under maintenance for the whole October. During this time, only elevators no. 2 and 4 will be available. We know that you may have to wait longer with only half of the elevators operating, but please understand that regular maintenance is essential to the safety of elevators. If you have any questions, please reach us at 1234-5678.

---

21. What is the main purpose of the memorandum?
    A. To encourage using elevators
    B. To announce some repair work
    C. To stay in contact with the residents
    D. To raise awareness about elevator safety

22. According to the memorandum, which of the following is true?
    A. There are four elevators in the building.
    B. Some residents oppose the maintenance.
    C. Residents cannot use elevators in October.
    D. There were some safety issues with the elevators.

第1回
第2回
第3回
第4回
第5回
第6回
第7回
第8回
第9回
第10回

From:	stanleywilson@email.com.tw
To:	alleystinson@awesomefurniture.com
Subject:	Purchase order

Attachment: purchase_items.pdf

Dear Ms. Stinson,

I am writing this email to tell you that I recently bought a new house and decided to purchase some furniture from your store. Please check the document I have attached. I listed the items I need and calculated the total cost. I also included the sizes of the rooms, so please check if the items would fit in. I hope the shipment can be delivered before April 25 because I have a business trip at the end of the month. Please let me know if it is possible.

By the way, I am a member of your reward program, so I would like to know if I can get a discount on this purchase. Thank you for your help!

Stanley Wilson

23. Why does Mr. Wilson write this email?
    A. To make a purchase
    B. To make a complaint
    C. To renew his membership
    D. To consult an interior professional

24. According to this email, which of the following is **NOT** true?
    A. Mr. Wilson wants to buy some furniture because he bought a new house.
    B. Mr. Wilson will go on a business trip in the middle of the month.
    C. Ms. Stinson needs to check the sizes of the items that Mr. Wilson wants to buy.
    D. The store has a reward program for some customers.

25. What information is **NOT** provided in the attached document?
    A. Room sizes
    B. Items to be purchased
    C. The amount of the order
    D. The purchasing price of the house

第 1 回
第 2 回
第 3 回
第 4 回
第 5 回
第 6 回
第 7 回
第 8 回
第 9 回
第 10 回

Questions 26-28 are based on information provided in the following advertisement and email.

Designers Wanted

Giant Design Group is looking for graphic designers with brilliant ideas. If you meet the following requirements and are interested in this opportunity, we encourage you to apply.
- At least bachelor's degree in art / design / multimedia / information technology
- At least 2 years of experience in art or design-related industries
- Proficiency in graphic design software

In addition to the requirements listed above, the following skills are not required but would be a plus for this position.
- Good communication skills, preferably with experiences in communicating with clients
- Skills of social media management

Successful candidates will be responsible for:
- Creating graphic contents for clients such as publisher, advertisers, etc.
- Creating visual materials for our social media accounts

Please send your résumé and portfolio to recruits@giantdesign.com. Thank you for considering joining our team!

From:	chloelin0617@email.com.tw
To:	recruits@giantdesign.com
Subject:	Application for the graphic designer position

Attachment: resume.pdf, portfolio_chloe.pdf

To whom it may concern,

Hi, I've seen the job advertisement on your website, and I would like to apply for the position of graphic designer. I graduated from Department of Art and Graphic Design of New Jersey University in 2018 and have worked in two design agencies since then. I am also responsible for maintaining the Facebook page of my current agency. Attached are my résumé and portfolio. Please contact me should you have any questions. Thank you.

Sincerely yours,
Chloe Lin

26. What is true about the job opening?
    A. The company is looking for software designers.
    B. Applicants for the position must have a college degree.
    C. Those who have worked in a publisher has a better chance of being hired.
    D. The job does not involve communicating with clients.

27. What can we infer about Chloe?
    A. She just graduated from university.
    B. She is working in Facebook.
    C. She is the spokesperson of her agency.
    D. She has changed jobs once.

28. To be considered a qualified applicant, what additional information should Chloe provide?
    A. Her educational background
    B. Her job experience
    C. Her computer skills
    D. Her résumé and portfolio

第 1 回
第 2 回
第 3 回
第 4 回
第 5 回
第 6 回
第 7 回
第 8 回
第 9 回
第 10 回

Questions 29-32

Are you sensitive towards other people's emotions and the environment around you? Do you feel uncomfortable in a crowded place that requires you to talk and socialize with people? Then it is likely you are a highly sensitive person (HSP). This term was invented in the mid-1990s by psychologists Elaine Aron and her husband Arthur Aron. They have been researching on highly sensitive people for a long time. According to the Arons and their colleagues, HSPs make up about 15-20% of the population.

A trait of HSPs is thinking more deeply than average people. They think about the consequences thoroughly before taking action, yet such a deep thinking process is easily deemed "overthinking". Another trait is being easily stressed by influences in the environment. For example, when they sense that someone is watching, they may have problem performing a task they are familiar with. They do things perfectly well when they are alone at home, but gets too nervous to do so in public.

Because of our culture of preferring positive and active personalities, being an HSP may be misunderstood as having a disease or disorder, but it is actually a natural part of who they are. Just like there are introverted and extroverted people, there are HSPs and those who are not. Next time when you find someone is an HSP, try to be more understanding and considerate of their sensitivity.

29. What is the main purpose of this article?
    A. To introduce a disease
    B. To clarify a personality type
    C. To encourage people to think more
    D. To teach people how to do research

30. What is true about the research on HSPs?
    A. The concept of HSP is developed in the past decade.
    B. The term HSP was created by a psychologist couple.
    C. It has been a long time since HSPs were last studied.
    D. Researchers find that HSPs are very rare.

31. According to the article, what is true about HSPs?
    A. They usually think twice before doing something.
    B. They do not care about how people think of them.
    C. They cannot do things well when they are alone.
    D. They want attention from people.

32. According to the article, what is a common misunderstanding about HSPs?
    A. They are born this way.
    B. They are highly talented.
    C. They lack depth in their thoughts.
    D. They just think too much.

第1回
第2回
第3回
第4回
第5回
第6回
第7回
第8回
第9回
第10回

Do you play video games? If so, you may already know what virtual reality (VR) is. Today, when we talk about VR experience, we usually mean wearing a VR headset. It consists of a screen in front of the eyes, and sometimes includes additional sensors or controllers to allow the user to interact with the virtual environment. With such features, the user will feel that they are immersed in the virtual world.

You may be under the impression that VR technology is just about gaming, but it has also been applied in many other fields. With VR technology, for example, students can attend virtual classes and interact with their teachers and classmates without traveling to school. For people who are physically challenged, they may also see a doctor and get proper medical treatment with the help of VR. The applications of VR have gone beyond what we could imagine in the past.

VR has already proved to be beneficial in many aspects in our life. With continued research and development, we can expect VR to play a significant role in many more fields and industries in the future.

33. Based on the article, what is true about VR technology?
    A. It was first invented by game designers.
    B. It takes some devices to experience it.
    C. It is not really useful in real life.
    D. It is a fully mature technology.

34. Which of the following is **NOT** mentioned as a field where VR can be applied?
    A. Gaming
    B. Education
    C. Tourism
    D. Health care

35. What is the author's thought about VR?
    A. Its usages are very predictable.
    B. It can improve the quality of human life.
    C. It is likely that people will abuse it.
    D. We should not rely on it all the time.

TEST 05

GEPT

全民英檢

中級初試

題目本

本測驗分四部分，全為四選一之選擇題，共 35 題，作答時間約 30 分鐘。

第一部分：看圖辨義

共 5 題，試題冊上有數幅圖畫，每一圖畫有 1~3 個描述該圖的題目，每題請聽光碟放音機播出題目以及四個英語敘述之後，選出與所看到的圖畫最相符的答案，每題只播出一遍。

例：（看）

（聽）

Look at the picture. What is the woman doing?

A. She is looking at a sculpture.

B. She is appreciating a painting.

C. She is picking up a handbag.

D. She is entering a museum.

正確答案為 B。

聽力測驗第一部分自本頁開始。

A. Question 1

Dallas Restaurant

Fast Food

BBQ Chicken	$18
Honey Chicken	$20
Hawaiian Pizza	$25

Drinks

Grape Soda	$10
Coffee	$7.5
Orange Juice	$11

B. Questions 2 and 3

FLASH BEATS FESTIVAL

SATURDAY, 18 AUGUST
FREE ENTRY

Featuring
Rattling Sticks
and many other local bands

Location:
Mapleton Public Park

*In case of rain, the event will be canceled.

C. Questions 4 and 5

Billy's Real Estate
FOR SALE

Perfect for families with children and pets

$700,000

- 2 Bedrooms
- 3 Bathrooms
- 1 Guest Room
- 1 Dining Room
- 1 Swimming Pool

Contact us for further info
123-456-7890

service@billysrealestate.com

第二部分：問答

共 10 題，每題請聽光碟放音機播出一英語問句或直述句之後，從試題冊上 A、B、C、D 四個回答或回應中，選出一個最適合者作答。每題只播出一遍。

例：（聽）Now that we've come to Kenting, we should try water sports.

（看）A. You can try harder next time.

B. Yes. I'm on the way there.

C. That sounds exciting to me.

D. We are coming in an hour.

正確答案為 C。

6. A. Yes. The hat was crushed.

B. Of course. It was terrifying.

C. No. I didn't see it coming.

D. Did anyone hit you?

7. A. I've seen actors on stage in theaters.

B. A quality film can make my day, too.

C. I can see the movie is well-received.

D. Which movie are you talking about?

8. A. Jim will be joining me for the meeting.

B. It was nice to meet him in person.

C. Yes. She is our new director.

D. I guess there are three of them.

9. A. He promised to solve the problem.

B. It seems to have a lot of potential.

C. I have no idea how he feels.

D. I don't think he will like it.

10. A. There's a record shop on the corner.

B. It's among the best-selling albums.

C. The convenience store has a copy machine.

D. You can find it on the street.

11. A. Yes. You can start tomorrow.
     B. It takes a week to recover.
     C. It's better late than never.
     D. You'd better hurry up, then.

12. A. History is not my thing.
     B. We have a family trip every year.
     C. My ancestors were from China.
     D. I know nothing about theories.

13. A. How can I help cheer you up?
     B. You don't need much to be happy.
     C. It's fine not to do well sometimes.
     D. Maybe you should see a doctor.

14. A. Can you ride a motorcycle?
     B. Not at all. You can use my car.
     C. Of course not. It's my day off today.
     D. I don't know you're taking drugs.

15. A. Will he become a musician?
     B. He can act in our stage play.
     C. It's too bad he got the flu.
     D. It's nice he can play games well.

第三部分：簡短對話

共 10 題，每題請聽光碟放音機播出一段對話及一個相關的問題後，從試題冊上 A、B、C、D 四個選項中選出一個最適合者作答。每段對話及問題只播出一遍。

例：（聽）（Woman）Excuse me. Does the next train go to the airport?

（Man）　　No. Actually, this is the high speed rail station. You should go to the airport MRT station nearby to get to the airport.

（Woman）Thank you for letting me know. This is my first time taking a train to the airport, so I didn't notice that.

Question:　What happened to the woman?

（看）A. She missed her train.

B. She got on the wrong train.

C. She went to the wrong station.

D. Her flight has already left.

正確答案為 C。

16. A. Being a transfer student.
    B. The way he talks.
    C. His fear of strangers.
    D. His teacher's words.

17. A. A take-out meal.
    B. A cell phone.
    C. A phone case.
    D. A cartoon character figure.

18. A. The man.
    B. The woman.
    C. Both of them.
    D. Neither of them.

19. A. Find a lost file.
    B. Revise the proposal.
    C. Know about the schedule.
    D. Suggest a solution.

20. A. At a museum.
    B. At a restaurant.
    C. At a theme park.
    D. At an office building.

21. A. He recently works at night.
    B. He is feeling anxious.
    C. He drinks too much coffee.
    D. He does not exercise.

22. A. Prices.
    B. Portion sizes.
    C. Healthy menus.
    D. Distance.

23. A. The neighbor upstairs.
    B. The security guard.
    C. The police.
    D. The building management.

24. **Bubble Tea Shops Review**

	Prices	Drinks	Desserts
Rando's	✕	★★	★
Bestie	✕	★★	✕
Pop Up	★	★	★
Louise	✕	★	✕

★★ Excellent ★ Satisfactory
✕ Poor

    A. Rando's.
    B. Bestie.
    C. Pop Up.
    D. Louise.

25. **Sam's Habit Tracker / July**

Date	1	2	3	4	5
Exercise for 30 minutes	○	○	●	○	○
Eat enough vegetables	○	●	●	●	○
Learn German	●	●	○	○	○

    A. July 1.
    B. July 2.
    C. July 3.
    D. July 4.

第四部分：簡短談話

共 10 題，每題請聽光碟放音機播出一段談話及一個相關的問題後，從試題冊上 A、B、C、D 四個選項中選出一個最適合者作答。每段談話及問題只播出一遍。

例：（聽）Teenagers can easily feel hurt in their social lives. When they have difficulty making friends, they may feel worried about going to school. Even if they are popular at school, they may be persuaded to do things they don't like, such as smoking or drinking, under peer pressure. The stress of fitting in can eventually make them mentally ill.

Question: According to the speaker, what makes a teenager try smoking even though they are not interested?

（看）A. Parents' complaint.
B. Friends' persuasion.
C. Romantic relationship.
D. Academic pressure.

正確答案為 B。

26. A. Friends.
    B. Mother and son.
    C. Teacher and student.
    D. Employer and employee.

27. A. A product.
    B. A factory.
    C. Sales performance.
    D. Marketing strategies.

28. A. He hit someone when driving.
    B. He knows how to dance.
    C. He will stay in hospital.
    D. He is leaving a hotel.

29. A. It enhances one's social skills.
    B. It does not require any equipment.
    C. It encourages real-world interactions.
    D. It shows people's real expressions.

30. A. It went out of order.
    B. It was stolen outside.
    C. It was put in some wrong place.
    D. It was switched with another.

第 1 回
第 2 回
第 3 回
第 4 回
第 5 回
第 6 回
第 7 回
第 8 回
第 9 回
第 10 回

31. A. Comedy performance.
    B. Street fair.
    C. Offering of free drinks.
    D. Concert.

32. A. She got a wrong order.
    B. Its food is of low quality.
    C. It offers few choices.
    D. It does not respond to
       complaints.

33. A. Physical health.
    B. Mental well-being.
    C. Professional performance.
    D. Financial situation.

34.

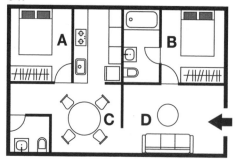

    A. Room A.
    B. Room B.
    C. Room C.
    D. Room D.

35.

	Tue.	Wed.	Thu.	Fri.
Weather				
Temp. (°C)	9-14	20-21	23-27	21-25

    A. Tuesday.
    B. Wednesday.
    C. Thursday.
    D. Friday.

本測驗分三部分，全為四選一之選擇題，共 35 題，作答時間 45 分鐘。

第一部分：詞彙

共 10 題，每題含一個空格。請由試題冊上的四個選項中選出最適合題意的字或詞作答。

1. The manager asked the team members to _____ a strategy at the meeting to beat their competitors.
   A. organize
   B. reveal
   C. execute
   D. devise

2. Those who are _____ of facts tend to believe fake news and false claims.
   A. aware
   B. tolerant
   C. convinced
   D. ignorant

3. This exhibition shows the artist's _____ of style through different periods.
   A. violation
   B. ambition
   C. destination
   D. evolution

4. Many older songs conclude by gradually _____, rather than having a distinct ending.
   A. taking off
   B. settling down
   C. fading out
   D. slipping away

5. Regularly expressing appreciation for each other can strengthen the emotional _____ between partners.
   A. bond
   B. dip
   C. gap
   D. impact

6. The _____ painted the sky with bursts of light and sound, impressing thousands of spectators.
   A. painter
   B. opera
   C. sunset
   D. fireworks

7. When the earthquake hit, the train was stopped to _____ the safety of all passengers.
   A. approve   B. ensure
   C. stress   D. research

8. A lot of species went _____ because they could not adapt to the sudden change of local climate.
   A. resistant   B. productive
   C. influential   D. extinct

9. The government is _____ money, so it cannot but shut down some services.
   A. doing away with   B. running out of
   C. looking down on   D. checking up on

10. I haven't met Cynthia for many years, so I spent some extra time _____ with her at the class reunion.
    A. getting even   B. carrying on
    C. catching up   D. putting up

第二部分：段落填空

共 10 題，包括二個段落，每個段落各含 5 個空格。請由試題冊上四個選項中選出最適合題意的字或詞作答。

Questions 11-15

Crop circles are patterns that have been found in fields of crops, often appearing overnight. Many people believe that they are the work of aliens or other supernatural forces, __(11)__ others claim that they are created by humans using ropes and boards. One may be under the impression that __(12)__, but in fact, there are numerous cases reported every year around the world. In 2002, a crop __(13)__ with over 400 circles was found in a field in the UK. It was so __(14)__ that many considered it could only be created by some unknown beings. The origin and meaning of crop circles will remain a mystery unless more evidence is revealed to help us __(15)__ them.

11. A. while
    B. because
    C. since
    D. if

12. A. crop circles are rarely found
    B. people do not understand crop circles
    C. it takes a lot of effort to make crop circles
    D. crop circles should be discussed case by case

13. A. confusion
    B. expansion
    C. formation
    D. occasion

14. A. complex
    B. genuine
    C. identical
    D. obvious

15. A. come up with
    B. make sense of
    C. look up to
    D. be true to

第 1 回
第 2 回
第 3 回
第 4 回
第 5 回
第 6 回
第 7 回
第 8 回
第 9 回
第 10 回

Questions 16-20

Remote work has become part of modern work culture. _(16)_ going to the office, remote workers can work from home, saving time and money spent on commuting. However, some _(17)_ come along with working from home. It can make it hard to separate work from personal life, potentially damaging _(18)_. Also, its nature of _(19)_ can create obstacles for teamwork. Some also feel that it takes more _(20)_ to stay efficient when there is no one watching.

16. A. instead of
    B. in addition to
    C. before
    D. in spite of

17. A. alternatives
    B. challenges
    C. equivalents
    D. guarantees

18. A. neighborhoods
    B. professions
    C. relationships
    D. substances

19. A. reducing time lost to
       commuting
    B. encouraging employees to
       work longer hours
    C. allowing employees to work in
       different places
    D. putting emphasis on outcomes
       rather than work hours

20. A. self-awareness
    B. self-confidence
    C. self-discipline
    D. self-improvement

第三部分：閱讀理解

共 15 題，包括數篇短文，每篇短文後有 2~4 個相關問題。請由試題冊上四個選項中選出最適合者作答。

Questions 21-22

Notice

Please be noted that the City Museum will be temporarily closed from January 16th to February 28th and is scheduled to reopen the first week of March. When the City Museum reopens, the addition of new spaces and restaurants will enhance the visitor experience. On the eve of the reopening day, there will be a celebration event where invited guests can get a glimpse of the brand-new museum. For information, please visit our website and Facebook page.

---

21. Why will the City Museum be closed?
    A. To hold a special event
    B. To be turned into a restaurant
    C. To make some repairs
    D. To improve its facilities

22. What is true about the event?
    A. It is open to the public.
    B. It will be held on March 1st.
    C. It allows some to take a look at the museum.
    D. The restaurants will serve some food during the event.

第1回
第2回
第3回
第4回
第5回
第6回
第7回
第8回
第9回
第10回

Dear Legacy Appliances,

I am writing to express my disappointment with your washing machine. Despite only being in use for a few months, the machine is not working well. On multiple occasions, I have found that the machine makes strange noises and shake intensely during operation. The only way to stop the quake is to take the plug out.

Your service team has sent technicians to fix the machine for three times, but the problem persists. I am extremely unhappy with the quality of this product and the inconvenience it has caused me. I expect better from the brand that I have been a loyal customer to. If I cannot have my money back, at least I want the machine replaced.

Thank you for your attention to this matter. I look forward to hearing back from you soon enough.

Sincerely,
Jackie Wu

23. What is the purpose of this letter?
    A. To cancel a purchase
    B. To complain about product quality
    C. To make an inquiry about a product
    D. To express gratitude to the service team

24. What is wrong with the washing machine?
    A. It is difficult to operate.
    B. Some parts of it are missing.
    C. It fails to function properly.
    D. It ruins the clothes put in.

25. What is true about Ms. Wu?
    A. She has purchased other items from this company before.
    B. She expects to have her money back instead of a replacement.
    C. She bought the washing machine online.
    D. She was hurt while using the washing machine.

第1回
第2回
第3回
第4回
第5回
第6回
第7回
第8回
第9回
第10回

Invitation

Mr. Jeffery Hendrick

You are warmly invited to join us for a Thanksgiving party.
Date: November 23
Time: 7 p.m. - 10 p.m.
Location: Grand Hotel

We would like to thank those who have participated in our international volunteer program in the past year, so we hope you come and enjoy roast turkey and other Thanksgiving dishes with your fellows. We also hope you would consider applying for the program next year, which will start from February.

Please RSVP by Nov. 12th to events@oedorganization.org, specifying the number of guests you will be bringing.

OED Organization

From:	jeffery_hendrick@celtmail.com
To:	events@oedorganization.org
Subject:	RSVP for Thanksgiving Party - Jeffery Hendrick

Dear staff at OED,

Thank you so much for the invitation. I gladly accept your invitation and will bring two people with me: my girlfriend Lisa and my friend Luke. Lisa has signed up for your program next year, but she has never been a volunteer before, so she wants to take this chance to know about what we do.

By the way, I have talked to Luke about my experience participating in your program before, and he shows genuine interest in your organization. Luke is an expert in agriculture & urban planning. He is working for the government at the moment, but he aims to serve a higher purpose in an NGO. I would like to introduce him to you at the party, and I believe his humorous nature will make him a good addition to your organization.

Warm Regards,
Jeffery Hendrick

26. Who does OED invite to its Thanksgiving party?
    A. Its volunteers.
    B. Its sponsors.
    C. Its clients.
    D. Its employees.

27. What is true about Lisa?
    A. She is Luke's girlfriend.
    B. She will attend the party alone.
    C. She can start volunteering from February next year.
    D. She has participated the same program with Jeffery before.

28. What is Luke planning to do?
    A. Change jobs
    B. Be a public servant
    C. Become a volunteer
    D. Start his own business

第1回
第2回
第3回
第4回
第5回
第6回
第7回
第8回
第9回
第10回

Questions 29-31

Frozen, a 2013 animated film produced by Walt Disney Animation Studios, follows the story of a princess named Elsa, who was born with the power to create and control ice and snow. Elsa's power brings joy as she and her sister, Anna, get to enjoy an icy world that belongs to them in their childhood. However, as the power grows out of control, Elsa also struggles to conceal this abnormal aspect of herself in front of others. In the end, she runs away from the kingdom fearing one day she might accidentally hurt those she loves, and that is when Anna goes on a journey into the unknown, helping her sister confront her fears.

Frozen has received positive opinions around the world and became a huge commercial success, earning over $1.2 billion at the box office and becoming one of the highest-grossing(收入最高的) animated films of all time. The two main characters, Elsa and Anna, are also seen as Disney's new icons. For some reason, however, they are not included in the official list of Disney princesses, who are a selection of female main characters that have royal ties or are known for heroic deeds (e.g. Mulan). Some say that Elsa and Anna don't qualify as Disney princesses as they have both become queens. Others claim that an official Disney princess needs an animal partner of their own, while Olaf, Elsa and Anna's magical snowman, is not even a living being. Still others are of the opinion that as far as business value is concerned, *Frozen* is such a huge brand in its own right. Parting Elsa and Anna from the other Disney princesses will be a wiser choice in business.

29. Which of the following is the best title for this article?
    A. Elsa and Anna: Disney's New Icons that Rock the World
    B. What Does It Take to Be a Disney Princess?
    C. Accepting Yourself: The Values Behind *Frozen*'s Success
    D. Discovering *Frozen*'s Life Lessons

30. How does Elsa feel when her magical power becomes hard to manage?
    A. Surprised
    B. Furious
    C. Unsure
    D. Delighted

31. According to the article, what is a requirement for Disney princesses?
    A. Appearing in a popular Disney movie
    B. Having royal status in a Disney movie
    C. Becoming a queen in the end of a movie
    D. Generating high sales with their goods

第1回
第2回
第3回
第4回
第5回
第6回
第7回
第8回
第9回
第10回

Questions 32-35

The online dating industry has seen itself growing in popularity in the past five years. Compared with meeting new friends at physical meet-ups, dating apps allow one to filter and select users more efficiently, and have thus become a preferable way of developing relationships for many people.

However, dating apps can also pose some risks. One of the major risks of dating apps is the possibility of being matched with frauds (騙子), who fake their identity and try to cheat other users out of their money. Frauds may use lies such as claiming an urgent need for money due to a crisis or offering information about a highly profitable investment. If you fall for these techniques and send them money, your bank account could be drained, and then you may never hear from them again.

Another risk of using dating apps is the higher chance of encountering inappropriate or offensive behavior. Though most apps allow users to report harassment or abuse, the fundamental reason behind such behavior is never solved. Being able to interact with others behind their phone screens, some users become offensive in ways they dare not try in person. Only when everyone learns to respect boundaries and exhibit good manners online will there be a safer digital environment for users.

Overall, it is important to be aware of the risks and take steps to protect yourself when using dating apps. While they can be a convenient and efficient way to meet new people, exercising caution and common sense remains crucial to ensure your safety. For example, it is advisable to avoid exposing sensitive personal information to people you have never met in person. By being careful online, you can have a safer experience while using dating apps.

32. According to the article, why do many people begin to use online dating apps?
    A. They can avoid people they are not interested in.
    B. They can choose not to expose some personal information.
    C. They can make friends with people experienced in investing.
    D. They do not need to pay any fee while using the services.

33. What is **NOT** a characteristic of online frauds mentioned in the article?
    A. They make up their identity.
    B. They pretend to solve people's crises.
    C. They provide fake investments.
    D. They disappear after getting money.

34. Which of the following is a function of dating apps mentioned in the article?
    A. Transferring money online
    B. Detecting frauds in real time
    C. Reporting inappropriate behavior
    D. Recommending dating spots

35. In order to use dating apps safely, what does the author recommend to do?
    A. Lie about one's own identity
    B. Try more aggressive ways of interacting
    C. Be cautious about sharing private details
    D. Only meet those who look less attractive

TEST 06

GEPT
全民英檢
中級初試

題目本

本測驗分四部分,全為四選一之選擇題,共 35 題,作答時間約 30 分鐘。

第一部分:看圖辨義

共 5 題,試題冊上有數幅圖畫,每一圖畫有 1~3 個描述該圖的題目,每題請聽光碟放音機播出題目以及四個英語敘述之後,選出與所看到的圖畫最相符的答案,每題只播出一遍。

例:(看)

(聽)

Look at the picture. What is the woman doing?

A. She is looking at a sculpture.

B. She is appreciating a painting.

C. She is picking up a handbag.

D. She is entering a museum.

正確答案為 B。

聽力測驗第一部分自本頁開始。

A. Question 1

Johnson's Clinic
Medical Checkup Packages

Item	Basic	Advanced	Premier
Blood pressure	●	●	●
Chest X-ray	●	●	●
Blood sugar		●	●
Liver function test		●	●
Kidney function test			●
Printed report	●	●	●
Price	**$119**	**$159**	**$199**

第1回
第2回
第3回
第4回
第5回
第6回
第7回
第8回
第9回
第10回

B. Questions 2 and 3

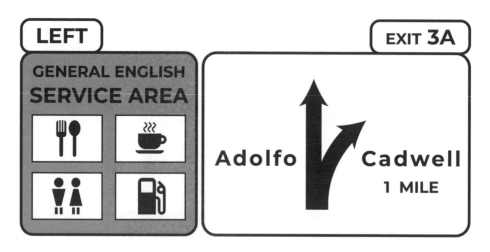

C. Questions 4 and 5

Global Village Adventure Land
Ticket Prices

Day / Hour	Regular	Children (<12) / Elderly (65+)	Group of 10+ (per person)
Weekday	$50	$40	$20
Weekend / Holiday	$90	$60	$30
Late entry (every day after 16:00)	$30	$10	$5

第二部分：問答

共 10 題，每題請聽光碟放音機播出一英語問句或直述句之後，從試題冊上 A、B、C、D 四個回答或回應中，選出一個最適合者作答。每題只播出一遍。

例：（聽）Now that we've come to Kenting, we should try water sports.
  （看）A. You can try harder next time.
    B. Yes. I'm on the way there.
    C. That sounds exciting to me.
    D. We are coming in an hour.

正確答案為 C。

6. A. Don't let likes define your self-worth.
   B. There really aren't many people like you.
   C. Spend more time browsing social media.
   D. Other people's opinions do matter.

7. A. Grace Stevenson is a famous model.
   B. We don't do role playing at work.
   C. I appreciate my manager's leadership style.
   D. I respect my mother's attitude toward life.

8. A. No. I prefer to volunteer my time.
   B. No. I only do it monthly.
   C. Yes. I donate blood regularly.
   D. Yes. I used to help an orphanage before.

9. A. Have you tried the new dog treats?
   B. How can you hate such cute creatures?
   C. Gradual exposure to them is necessary.
   D. You should fight back when they come.

10. A. Sure, what can I pick for you?
    B. No, it's an inconvenient truth.
    C. Okay, but I need to know when.
    D. Of course, you're right about it.

11. A. The effect of financial regulation.
    B. Some economical ways of grocery shopping.
    C. Actually, it's not my major.
    D. Why are you sick of economics?

12. A. I have seen better days.
    B. Yes, you should wear a coat.
    C. It will begin to rain on Friday.
    D. It'll be cold for at least a week.

13. A. Not really. Audience makes me nervous.
    B. I'm afraid it's too far to deliver.
    C. Sure. I'm ready for tomorrow.
    D. I have no problem speaking in class.

14. A. Make a detailed travel plan in advance.
    B. Try to follow their customs when you can.
    C. Make sure to wear warm clothes.
    D. Just be yourself and they'll see.

15. A. Who did you see perform?
    B. What's your taste in music?
    C. I love pop music, too.
    D. You must be screaming all the time.

第三部分：簡短對話

共 10 題，每題請聽光碟放音機播出一段對話及一個相關的問題後，從試題冊上 A、B、C、D 四個選項中選出一個最適合者作答。每段對話及問題只播出一遍。

例：（聽）（Woman） Excuse me. Does the next train go to the airport?

（Man） No. Actually, this is the high speed rail station. You should go to the airport MRT station nearby to get to the airport.

（Woman） Thank you for letting me know. This is my first time taking a train to the airport, so I didn't notice that.

Question: What happened to the woman?

（看）A. She missed her train.
　　　B. She got on the wrong train.
　　　C. She went to the wrong station.
　　　D. Her flight has already left.

正確答案為 C。

16. A. A wedding reception.
　　B. A farewell party.
　　C. A business dinner party.
　　D. An award ceremony.

17. A. The word processing software.
　　B. The operating system.
　　C. Fixing a screen.
　　D. Designing a document.

18. A. History of Europe.
　　B. Travel to Europe.
　　C. European literature.
　　D. A course about Europe.

19. A. Cave exploration.
　　B. Beautiful landscape.
　　C. Souvenir shopping.
　　D. Water sports.

20. A. The rental agreement cannot be renewed.
　　B. The rent keeps going higher.
　　C. He has a higher pay now.
　　D. It is his long-time dream.

21. A. He got a flu.
　　B. He has some side effects.
　　C. His whole body is aching.
　　D. He does not do well at school.

22. A. Organize events.
    B. Sweep their rooms.
    C. Design their homes.
    D. Get rid of unneeded things.

23. A. Movie-going.
    B. New clothes.
    C. Food ingredients.
    D. Eating out.

24.

Train	Destination	Time	Expected
1238	Taichung	10:39	On Time
1362	Kaohsiung	10:45	Delayed 10 min.
1364	Kaohsiung	11:08	On Time
1240	Taichung	11:15	Delayed 7 min.

Time Now 10:37

    A. Train 1238.
    B. Train 1362.
    C. Train 1364.
    D. Train 1240.

25.

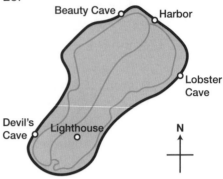

    A. Devil's Cave.
    B. Beauty Cave.
    C. Lobster Cave.
    D. The lighthouse.

第四部分：簡短談話

共 10 題，每題請聽光碟放音機播出一段談話及一個相關的問題後，從試題冊上 A、B、C、D 四個選項中選出一個最適合者作答。每段談話及問題只播出一遍。

例：（聽）Teenagers can easily feel hurt in their social lives. When they have difficulty making friends, they may feel worried about going to school. Even if they are popular at school, they may be persuaded to do things they don't like, such as smoking or drinking, under peer pressure. The stress of fitting in can eventually make them mentally ill.

Question: According to the speaker, what makes a teenager try smoking even though they are not interested?

（看）A. Parents' complaint.
B. Friends' persuasion.
C. Romantic relationship.
D. Academic pressure.

正確答案為 B。

26. A. Quarreling with her partner.
    B. Lack of communication.
    C. Signs of depression.
    D. Difference of habits.

27. A. An accountant.
    B. A researcher.
    C. A consultant.
    D. A farmer.

28. A. Protective gear.
    B. Creatures in the river.
    C. The speed of the current.
    D. Riverside scenery.

29. A. This afternoon.
    B. This evening.
    C. Tomorrow.
    D. The day after tomorrow.

30. A. Rent a car.
    B. Buy a tent.
    C. Buy a blanket.
    D. Buy a sleeping bag.

31. A. Coping with emotions.
    B. Doing exercise.
    C. Developing hobbies.
    D. Communicating with others.

32. A. Buy a ticket.
    B. Go to the train station.
    C. Bring their own seats.
    D. Talk to the front desk.

33. A. Coffee capsules.
    B. Coffee beans.
    C. Water.
    D. Sugar.

34.
ASIA TRAVEL PLANS

	Basic		Advanced	
	5 days **$20**	**10 days** **$30**	**5 days** **$40**	**10 days** **$60**
Free Phone Call	×	10 min.	20 min.	40 min.
High Speed Data*	5GB	10GB	Unlimited	Unlimited

*Internet speed will be limited to 20Mbps when the allowance is used up.

    A. Basic 5 days.
    B. Basic 10 days.
    C. Advanced 5 days.
    D. Advanced 10 days.

35.

Movie Schedule	
Mandala Type: Sci-Fi 6:30 p.m. 9:00 p.m.	***Air Crush*** Type: Horror 6:00 p.m. 8:30 p.m.
Don't Look Down Type: Comedy 6:30 p.m. 9:00 p.m.	***You've Got Message*** Type: Romantic 6:00 p.m. 8:30 p.m.

    A. *Mandala.*
    B. *Air Crush.*
    C. *Don't Look Down.*
    D. *You've Got Message.*

本測驗分三部分，全為四選一之選擇題，共 35 題，作答時間 45 分鐘。

第一部分：詞彙

共 10 題，每題含一個空格。請由試題冊上的四個選項中選出最適合題意的字或詞作答。

1. Jennifer slipped on the wet floor and _____ down the stairs.
   A. stepped
   B. bounced
   C. tumbled
   D. knocked

2. The popular basketball player was suspended for a year after testing positive for a prohibited _____.
   A. formula
   B. movement
   C. revenge
   D. substance

3. Companies that _____ old business models risk falling behind their competitors.
   A. look forward to
   B. hold on to
   C. catch up with
   D. get away with

4. Music is a _____ language because it can be understood without translation.
   A. universal
   B. gorgeous
   C. continental
   D. regional

5. Those who have _____ points of view can easily fight, and it takes communication to come to a meaningful resolution.
   A. opposite
   B. defensive
   C. pessimistic
   D. halfway

6. Lemon juice and vinegar taste sour because they contain _____.
   A. acne
   B. atom
   C. acid
   D. liquor

7. _____-free beer allows people to enjoy the taste of beer even when they drive.
   A. alcohol
   B. flavor
   C. vapor
   D. moisture

8. Jacky turned off his phone and locked his room _____ he wouldn't be disturbed.
   A. as long as
   B. so that
   C. in case
   D. even though

9. Because the main _____ decided to stop funding, the famous marathon is at risk of not being held this year.
   A. interpreter
   B. intruder
   C. spectator
   D. sponsor

10. It was _____ of the player to hit his opponent and caused him serious injury in the game.
    A. brutal
    B. intimate
    C. sensitive
    D. vigorous

第二部分：段落填空

共 10 題，包括二個段落，每個段落各含 5 個空格。請由試題冊上四個選項中選出最適合題意的字或詞作答。

Questions 11-15

Aphasia is a kind of language ___(11)___ . Patients of aphasia ___(12)___ difficulty with speaking and reading. For example, the well-known actor Bruce Willis, who has been diagnosed with aphasia, became unable to remember and ___(13)___ his lines. ___(14)___ that aphasia affects one's language ability, it does not impact overall intelligence. Therefore, patients of aphasia can feel the pain of not being able to communicate normally. To make them feel more comfortable and to aid their communication abilities, it is advisable to ___(15)___ when we talk to them.

11. A. dilemma
    B. incident
    C. symptom
    D. disorder

12. A. suffer from
    B. inquire about
    C. throw out
    D. feel for

13. A. recite
    B. repeat
    C. declare
    D. clarify

14. A. With the consequence
    B. Despite the fact
    C. In view of the fact
    D. On top of

15. A. mock at the way they talk
    B. speak in a clear and simple way
    C. put up with their negative mood
    D. accept the situation and let it be

Questions 16-20

With more and more people choosing to pay with their phones, digital payment has proven to be ___(16)___ popular. One of the reasons is that digital payment can be done by simply tapping the phone or scanning a bar code, while cash and credit cards require ___(17)___ handling, which can be time-consuming. As a result, many retailers and service providers now accept digital payment, further ___(18)___ its popularity. Despite the fact that digital payment has been widely accepted, however, ___(19)___. For example, some users have complained about not being able to pay digitally due to Internet connection issues. To gain more users and win their trust, digital payment companies should ___(20)___ the problem and prevent it from happening again.

16. A. essentially
    B. properly
    C. hopefully
    D. increasingly

17. A. physical
    B. critical
    C. identical
    D. logical

18. A. contributing to
    B. corresponding to
    C. disagreeing with
    D. experimenting with

19. A. it is not always reliable
    B. some still prefer to use cash
    C. there are concerns about privacy
    D. not everyone knows how to use it

20. A. abide by
    B. sort out
    C. break down
    D. come up with

第三部分：閱讀理解

共 15 題，包括數篇短文，每篇短文後有 2~4 個相關問題。請由試題冊上四個選項中選出最適合者作答。

Questions 21-22

How to Handle Delicate Clothes

To make your clothes last longer and stay in better condition, check their wash tags to see if they need special care. Take the following steps if they require hand washing.

1. Fill a sink or bathtub with water and detergent. Make sure not to use water hotter than recommended on the tag.
2. Soak the clothes in the mixture and scrub gently.
3. Drain the sink or bathtub and refill it with clean water.
4. Rinse the clothes.
5. Repeat steps 3 and 4 until no detergent remains.

---

21. According to the article, what should one do before washing clothes by hand?
    A. Pour hot water
    B. Look at the wash tag
    C. Wash the sink with detergent
    D. Soak the clothes in pure detergent

22. What is true about the method of washing clothes introduced in the article?
    A. It is a harsh method to wash clothes.
    B. It uses less water than washing machines.
    C. It helps keep clothes in good shape.
    D. It can save time doing laundry.

第 1 回
第 2 回
第 3 回
第 4 回
第 5 回
第 6 回
第 7 回
第 8 回
第 9 回
第 10 回

Dear Admissions Committee,

I am writing to express my sincere interest in enrolling in the MBA program at your university. After researching MBA programs provided by different universities and knowing about your reputation and academic achievements, I am confident that your program is ideal for me.

As a recent university graduate with a top academic record, I am eager to develop my business and management skills to achieve my career goals. Currently, I am working as an intern at a prominent firm, where I have been able to improve my financial knowledge and problem-solving skills. However, I have also identified a gap in my professional knowledge. I believe I need to further advance my knowledge and ability to achieve success in the financial field.

Your MBA program, which emphasizes investment analysis and accounting, is precisely what I am seeking to address my professional weakness. Enclosed you will find my application form and all required paperwork. I am eagerly awaiting your positive response. Thank you for considering my application.

Yours Sincerely,
Lucas Williams

23. Why did Mr. Williams write this letter?
    A. To show his financial knowledge
    B. To apply for internship
    C. To request to study at a university
    D. To seek career counseling

24. What can we infer about Mr. Williams?
    A. He is recommended for admission to the university.
    B. He has done research on various universities.
    C. He is a graduate of accounting.
    D. He has no previous job experience.

25. What does Mr. Williams want to improve?
    A. Investment knowledge
    B. Account management
    C. Problem-solving skills
    D. Public relations skills

第1回
第2回
第3回
第4回
第5回
第6回
第7回
第8回
第9回
第10回

Questions 26-28 are based on information provided in the following article and email.

How to Tell if an Egg is Fresh

Eggs are regarded as one of the healthiest foods available. They are a good source of protein as well as important nutrients such as vitamin B6, B12, and D, which are important for brain development and bone health. Additionally, they may help with weight management because they can make you feel full for longer and eat less. However, if eggs are not stored properly, bacteria may enter and make you sick. Here are some methods for determining whether an egg is safe to eat.

Method	Sign of Freshness
Check the expiration date	Later than purchase date
Smell the egg	No bad smell
Look at the egg shell	Dry and not damaged
Put in a bowl of water	Sinking and laying on the side
Examine the egg white after cracking	Clear or slightly yellow but not pink

From:	CharlotteC@ggmail.com
To:	service@costcaresuper.com
Subject:	Suspected unfresh eggs

Dear Sir/Madam,

I am writing to inform you that I recently purchased a dozen eggs from CostCare Supermarket, and I suspect that they are not fresh. Their shells are quite dry, and when I put them in water, they float on the surface. Also, when I crack them, the egg white looks kind of yellow.

I would like to request that you address this issue as soon as possible, as I am concerned about the quality of your products. I would appreciate it if you could provide me with a refund. Thank you for your attention to this matter.

Sincerely,
Charlotte Carter

26. What is **NOT** a benefit of eggs mentioned in the article?
    A. Helping the brain to grow and mature
    B. Keeping bones in good condition
    C. Preventing the fat in food from being stored in one's body
    D. Reducing the possibility of over-eating.

27. What aspect of Ms. Carter's eggs shows that they may not be fresh?
    A. The dryness of their shells
    B. The way they look in water
    C. The color of their white
    D. The way they smell

28. What does Ms. Carter hope that CostCare Supermarket will do to address the problem?
    A. Pay her money back
    B. Provide her with new eggs
    C. Stop selling eggs as soon as possible
    D. Help its customers to notice the problem

Questions 29-31

Layoffs(裁員) are typically driven by business-related reasons such as budget constraints, a decline in sales, or changes in market conditions. These reasons are generally unrelated to individual employees' performance. Given the impact of layoffs on individuals and the broader community, it is important for companies to carefully consider all options before cutting its staff.

If a company decides that layoffs are necessary, it is crucial to handle the process properly. Employers should consult with labor and employment relations experts about legal issues involved, and learn about laws and regulations governing layoffs and collective bargaining agreements (集體談判協議). In addition to examining and deciding on the departments to be affected, following a fair and transparent process of selecting employees for layoff is also important.

While it is important to handle layoffs legally, perhaps the greatest challenge is managing the emotional impact on employees who are affected by the layoff. Knowing that they will lose their jobs, the employees may feel anxiety or panic. Therefore, employers should try to minimize the impact by providing advance notice and offering support such as severance pay (遣散費) and career counseling. By treating affected employees with respect, employers can maintain their reputation as being responsible and caring.

29. What is the article mainly about?
    A. The potential problems of layoffs
    B. The layoff policy of the government
    C. The ideal way of handling layoffs
    D. The importance of communication during a layoff

30. What is **NOT** a reason for layoffs mentioned in the article?
    A. Not having enough money to pay salaries
    B. Having worse company performance than before
    C. Business environment being different from the past
    D. Employees behaving in an unsatisfactory manner

31. What does the author consider to be the most difficult thing while laying off employees?
    A. Consulting experts
    B. Learning about laws and regulations
    C. Deciding who to lay off
    D. Preventing mental shock on employees

第1回
第2回
第3回
第4回
第5回
第6回
第7回
第8回
第9回
第10回

Questions 32-35

Physically attractive individuals, such as those with slender waists or appealing features, tend to be more recognized by society, and such a phenomenon has become even more prevalent in this age of social media. The overwhelming amount of photos and videos online showing ideal body images have influenced the way teenagers see themselves, often making them feel inferior in how they look.

For example, seeing that a smaller face with a straight nose is in trend nowadays, those who do not meet the standard may seek ways to "improve" their appearance, such as getting plastic surgery, which has seen a dramatic rise in recent years as a result of the pressure to fit in certain beauty standards.

It seems that many teenagers who choose to reshape their body parts through surgeries are more concerned about how others see them than how they see themselves. Some of them decide to do so because their appearance is negatively judged by their peers, and they expect to win some respect by changing it. However, there is no end in pursuing the ideal, and it turns out that some of them are never satisfied with the results and keep wanting more.

While plastic surgery can offer a quick fix to physical appearance, it is important to recognize that all surgeries carry some level of risk. The risks are higher for young people, whose bodies are still developing and maturing. Parents should educate their children on the potential risks of getting plastic surgery at a young age, and encourage them to carefully consider the long-term consequences of surgically changing their bodies.

32. Which of the following is the best title for this article?
    A. Plastic Surgery and Teenagers' Pursuit of Beauty
    B. How Social Media is Encouraging Body Positivity
    C. The Benefits of Plastic Surgery for Teenagers
    D. Why Beauty Standards are Important for Teenagers

33. What is a reason mentioned in the article that teenagers seek plastic surgery?
    A. Being encouraged by their peers
    B. Not getting praise from their parents
    C. Being teased about their body features
    D. Being mentally mature earlier than others

34. Based on the article, which of the following is **NOT** true?
    A. People with a thin waist are thought to have an ideal body shape.
    B. Plastic surgeries can make teenagers happy about themselves for a long time.
    C. It is more dangerous for young people to get plastic surgery than adults.
    D. Social media has significant impact on the self images of teenagers.

35. What is something the author suggests parents to tell their children about plastic surgery?
    A. There may be a legal problem.
    B. They cannot afford a surgery.
    C. Their bodies are not fully grown.
    D. It is too painful to go through.

第 1 回
第 2 回
第 3 回
第 4 回
第 5 回
第 6 回
第 7 回
第 8 回
第 9 回
第 10 回

TEST 07

**GEPT
全民英檢**

中級初試

題目本

本測驗分四部分，全為四選一之選擇題，共 35 題，作答時間約 30 分鐘。

第一部分：看圖辨義

共 5 題，試題冊上有數幅圖畫，每一圖畫有 1~3 個描述該圖的題目，每題請聽光碟放音機播出題目以及四個英語敘述之後，選出與所看到的圖畫最相符的答案，每題只播出一遍。

例：（看）

（聽）

Look at the picture. What is the woman doing?

A. She is looking at a sculpture.

B. She is appreciating a painting.

C. She is picking up a handbag.

D. She is entering a museum.

正確答案為 B。

聽力測驗第一部分自本頁開始。

A. Question 1

第1回
第2回
第3回
第4回
第5回
第6回
第7回
第8回
第9回
第10回

FRESH FRUITS

 4 for NT$100

 1 for NT$120

 4 for NT$120

 10 for NT$100

153

Welcome to **Teleport Plaza**

↑ Men's Fashion

↑ Movie Theater

→ Silky Beauty Salon

← Ichiban Japanese Restaurant

↩ Amazing Western Diner

C. Questions 4 and 5

Sally 's Weekly Planner

Monday	Tuesday	Wednesday	Thursday
	weekly photography class	play badminton	do the groceries

Friday	Saturday	Sunday	Notes
	yoga class	see a movie	

第二部分：問答

共 10 題，每題請聽光碟放音機播出一英語問句或直述句之後，從試題冊上 A、B、C、D 四個回答或回應中，選出一個最適合者作答。每題只播出一遍。

例： （聽）Now that we've come to Kenting, we should try water sports.

（看）　　A.　You can try harder next time.

　　　　　　B.　Yes. I'm on the way there.

　　　　　　C.　That sounds exciting to me.

　　　　　　D.　We are coming in an hour.

正確答案為 C。

6. A. That sounds like a great idea.
   B. Yeah. I think it's fantastic.
   C. No. I haven't heard the news report.
   D. No. What is the album's genre?

7. A. I'd like to, but I don't have time.
   B. I'm not really into abstract art.
   C. When will the exhibition start?
   D. They must be very realistic.

8. A. I like to watch movies.
   B. I'm afraid of being alone.
   C. I keep myself in shape.
   D. This game is really interesting.

9. A. Where can I find a laundry?
   B. I always like to do the chores.
   C. I got busy and didn't have time.
   D. Yes. I'm doing the laundry now.

10. A. You need to hide under a table.
    B. Take the elevator and go outside.
    C. You should be careful next time.
    D. It's better safe than sorry.

11.　A.　He feels at ease at work.
　　　B.　Maybe he's tired of complaining.
　　　C.　He can't just keep asking for more.
　　　D.　No wonder he went to bed early.

12.　A.　Can I leave a message for him?
　　　B.　Should I cancel my appointment?
　　　C.　What is the problem with him?
　　　D.　When did he leave his position?

13.　A.　I knew the weather would be nice.
　　　B.　Make sure to check the forecast.
　　　C.　Don't forget to bring a tent.
　　　D.　Where will you go hiking?

14.　A.　How long have you spent on it?
　　　B.　You can come again next month.
　　　C.　You should track your expenses.
　　　D.　Money can't buy everything.

15.　A.　He will promote it himself.
　　　B.　He doesn't like to pay attention.
　　　C.　He's not a fan of big gatherings.
　　　D.　He can be easily satisfied.

第三部分：簡短對話

共 10 題，每題請聽光碟放音機播出一段對話及一個相關的問題後，從試題冊上 A、B、C、D 四個選項中選出一個最適合者作答。每段對話及問題只播出一遍。

例：（聽）（Woman）Excuse me. Does the next train go to the airport?

（Man）No. Actually, this is the high speed rail station. You should go to the airport MRT station nearby to get to the airport.

（Woman）Thank you for letting me know. This is my first time taking a train to the airport, so I didn't notice that.

Question: What happened to the woman?

（看）A. She missed her train.

B. She got on the wrong train.

C. She went to the wrong station.

D. Her flight has already left.

正確答案為 C。

16. A. Seeing a doctor.
    B. Taking medicine.
    C. Getting a rapid test.
    D. Wearing a mask.

17. A. It is an action movie.
    B. Tom Cruise tried some difficult scenes.
    C. Tom Cruise looks great at his 60s.
    D. The woman wants to see it.

18. A. Its decorations.
    B. Its service staff.
    C. Its food.
    D. Its prices.

19. A. Stopping eating junk food.
    B. Eating a lot of vegetables.
    C. Quitting having food late at night.
    D. Recording what she eats.

20. A. He is not skilled enough.
    B. His teammates are weak.
    C. He has no luck at all.
    D. He cannot give directions.

21. A. The test was difficult.
    B. He did not work hard.
    C. He was not aware of the test.
    D. He did not learn from his mistakes.

22. A. Go hiking.
     B. Go mountain climbing.
     C. Play badminton.
     D. Play tennis.

23. A. She got hurt.
     B. She does not like practicing.
     C. Her instructor left.
     D. She has no talent.

24.

Art Museums in Tokyo

Museum	Exhibits	Closed
Museum of Contemporary Art	Modern art	Monday
Museum of Modern Art	Modern art	Tuesday
Nezu Museum	Traditional art and crafts	Monday
Suntory Museum	Traditional art and crafts	Tuesday

A. Museum of Contemporary Art.
B. Museum of Modern Art.
C. Nezu Museum.
D. Suntory Museum.

25.

Leadership and Teamwork Workshop

	Wednesday	Thursday
9:00-12:00	Session 1: Introduction to Leadership and Teamwork	Session 3: Building High-Performing Teams
12:00-14:00	Lunch Break	
14:00-17:00	Session 2: Effective Leadership and Decision-Making	Session 4: Cooperating with Colleagues the Right Way

A. Session 1.
B. Session 2.
C. Session 3.
D. Session 4.

第四部分：簡短談話

共 10 題，每題請聽光碟放音機播出一段談話及一個相關的問題後，從試題冊上 A、B、C、D 四個選項中選出一個最適合者作答。每段談話及問題只播出一遍。

例：（聽）Teenagers can easily feel hurt in their social lives. When they have difficulty making friends, they may feel worried about going to school. Even if they are popular at school, they may be persuaded to do things they don't like, such as smoking or drinking, under peer pressure. The stress of fitting in can eventually make them mentally ill.

Question: According to the speaker, what makes a teenager try smoking even though they are not interested?

（看）A. Parents' complaint.
B. Friends' persuasion.
C. Romantic relationship.
D. Academic pressure.

正確答案為 B。

26. A. It is preparing to fly.
    B. It is taking off.
    C. It is flying.
    D. It is landing.

27. A. Take a Spanish test.
    B. Submit her science project.
    C. Paint a watercolor painting.
    D. Go to school.

28. A. Software.
    B. Machinery.
    C. Home appliances.
    D. Consulting service.

29. A. It allows for cord-free operation.
    B. It can transfer data wirelessly.
    C. Its vacuuming power is stronger.
    D. It detects dirt automatically.

30. A. By watching GPTV.
    B. By visiting GPTV's website.
    C. By answering the result after the game.
    D. By going to the stadium in person.

第 1 回
第 2 回
第 3 回
第 4 回
第 5 回
第 6 回
第 7 回
第 8 回
第 9 回
第 10 回

31. A. To recommend ordering a purse.
    B. To invite her to see new stuff.
    C. To report the status of an order.
    D. To help her exchange a bag.

32. A. Listening.
    B. Speaking.
    C. Reading.
    D. Writing.

33. A. Award winners.
    B. Bride and groom.
    C. Childhood friends.
    D. University students.

34.

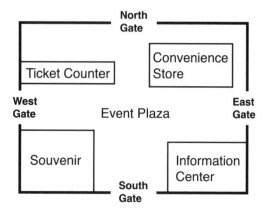

A. At the north gate.
B. At the east gate.
C. At the south gate.
D. At the west gate.

35.

Game	Price	Availability	Release Date
Super Sports	NT$1530	In stock	February 3
Maria's Cart	NT$1230	In stock	February 10
Star Playground	NT$1800	In stock	May 1
Poke the Monster	NT$2200	Sold out	May 15

A. Super Sports.
B. Maria's Cart.
C. Star Playground.
D. Poke the Monster.

本測驗分三部分，全為四選一之選擇題，共 35 題，作答時間 45 分鐘。

第一部分：詞彙

共 10 題，每題含一個空格。請由試題冊上的四個選項中選出最適合題意的字或詞作答。

1. We conduct regular customer surveys to ensure our products live up to their _____.
    A. expectations
    B. generations
    C. implications
    D. limitations

2. _____ government data, average manufacturing salary has been rising these years.
    A. According to
    B. Regardless of
    C. In return for
    D. In case of

3. The price of natural gas went up when Russia stopped _____ to European countries.
    A. extending
    B. exporting
    C. exposing
    D. expanding

4. The new company building is more convenient because it is _____ in the central business district.
    A. captured
    B. located
    C. observed
    D. installed

5. If we try to put ourselves _____, we can better understand their decisions.
    A. ahead of others
    B. on others' behalf
    C. out of others' league
    D. in others' shoes

6. Mr. Kitagawa is so _____ that everyone feels at home when visiting him.
    A. intellectual
    B. productive
    C. hospitable
    D. favorable

7. Balanced _____ and sufficient exercise can significantly contribute to the recovery after an illness.
    A. application
    B. nutrition
    C. recognition
    D. starvation

8. Researchers should conduct their studies and arrive at conclusions _____ evidence rather than subjective opinions.
    A. prior to
    B. based on
    C. at odds with
    D. at the expense of

9. After thoroughly investigating the accident, it became _____ that one of the cars was not functioning properly.
    A. distant
    B. formal
    C. peculiar
    D. obvious

10. Ben lied about his score to avoid being _____ by his mother.
    A. skipped
    B. charged
    C. hired
    D. scolded

第二部分：段落填空

共 10 題，包括二個段落，每個段落各含 5 個空格。請由試題冊上四個選項中選出最適合題意的字或詞作答。

Questions 11-15

During the pandemic years, __(11)__ . To prevent the spread of virus, distance learning became a widely adopted __(12)__ to traditional in-person education. However, the requirement for equipment such as computers and a reliable Internet connection formed a __(13)__ for some students, limiting their access to online classes. __(14)__ , some schools provided tablets and recorded lessons to students to help close the technology gap and ensure no one is left behind. After all, technological progress in education has little meaning if it is available only to a __(15)__ few.

11.　A. the method of school education changed significantly
　　B. the education industry was almost completely destroyed
　　C. every student benefited from the evolution of education
　　D. learning became impossible for most students

12.　A. apology
　　B. admission
　　C. alternative
　　D. agreement

13.　A. barrier
　　B. disorder
　　C. judgment
　　D. reaction

14.　A. Moreover
　　B. However
　　C. Otherwise
　　D. Therefore

15.　A. devoted
　　B. enclosed
　　C. fascinated
　　D. privileged

Questions 16-20

     As living spaces __(16)__ , it is now less favored to own every book physically. In contrast, e-books do not __(17)__ physical space and can be conveniently accessed anywhere using mobile devices. However, reading on a tablet or computer screen for extended periods can be uncomfortable, so e-readers with e-paper technology are becoming more and more popular among __(18)__ readers. Unlike traditional screens, e-paper does not need to be lit from the back. As a result, it provides a reading experience similar to reading from a printed page, __(19)__ . As e-readers become more cost-effective and within __(20)__ reach for a broader population, it is expected that e-books will be accepted by more people in the future.

16. A. choke
    B. drain
    C. loosen
    D. shrink

17. A. add to
    B. turn in
    C. take up
    D. set off

18. A. energetic
    B. pessimistic
    C. enthusiastic
    D. sympathetic

19. A. making it gentler on the eyes
    B. providing greater visual impact
    C. proving the value of physical books
    D. causing a mixed reaction among people

20. A. financial
    B. essential
    C. potential
    D. commercial

第三部分：閱讀理解

共 15 題，包括數篇短文，每篇短文後有 2~4 個相關問題。請由試題冊上四個選項中選出最適合者作答。

第 1 回
第 2 回
第 3 回
第 4 回
第 5 回
第 6 回
第 7 回
第 8 回
第 9 回
第 10 回

Questions 21-22

Notice

In light of the recent release of the new function in our intranet（內部網路）system, we have scheduled a training session to all employees on Friday afternoon. It will include detailed demonstrations and time for questions and answers, and we are offering both physical and online attendance options. If you are present in the office on that day, please join us in Room 416. Alternatively, for those working remotely, we will send the online meeting link 30 minutes prior to the scheduled time. Should you have any inquiries, please contact the information department. Thank you for your cooperation.

---

21. What is the main purpose of this notice?
    A. To introduce a new function
    B. To encourage using the intranet
    C. To inform of an educational session
    D. To recommend meeting online

22. According to the notice, which of the following is true?
    A. The new function of the intranet is yet to be released.
    B. Every employee should come to the office on Friday.
    C. Participants can ask about how to use the new function in the session.
    D. Employees will be given the link to the online meeting when it starts.

From:	Emilia Dallas <emiliadallas@joyeducation.com>
To:	Janice Wang <janicewang@geemail.com>
Subject:	Your subscription
Attachment:	Subscription_detail.pdf; plans.pdf

Dear Ms. Wang,

I am Emilia Dallas, the sales manager at Joy Education. I would like to express my gratitude for your participation in our program in the past year. I am writing to inform you that your subscription with Joy Education will be due next month. Before the due date, you have the opportunity to decide whether you would like to upgrade your current plan or maintain the existing one. We are also pleased to offer a discount that is only available to those who upgrade.

For complete details regarding your subscription, please refer to the attached document. Additionally, I have included a document introducing our plans for your reference.

We highly value your feedback and believe in continuously improving our services. Your class-taking experiences throughout the past year are highly valuable to us. We kindly request you to share your feedback and suggestions. At Joy Education, we are committed to listening and addressing every student's needs and concerns.

Thank you for your continued support and trust in Joy Education. We look forward to serving you in the coming year.

Sincerely,

Emilia Dallas
Sales Manager
Joy Education

23. Why did Ms. Dallas write this email?
    A. To attract a potential customer
    B. To encourage renewing a subscription
    C. To deal with a customer's complaints
    D. To provide a billing statement

24. According to this email, what can Ms. Wang do?
    A. Upgrade her plan with a discount
    B. Continue with her current plan at a lower price
    C. Refer a friend to get a benefit
    D. Cancel her subscription and get a refund

25. According to this email, which of the following is true?
    A. Ms. Dallas is new to her department.
    B. Ms. Dallas has provided a list of service plans.
    C. Ms. Wang is not satisfied with the service.
    D. Ms. Wang has written to Ms. Dallas before.

第1回
第2回
第3回
第4回
第5回
第6回
第7回
第8回
第9回
第10回

Questions 26-28 are based on information provided in the following ad and email.

Welcome to the Toy Expo!

Calling all toy collectors and parents seeking the coolest toys for their kids! Prepare to be amazed at the annual Toy Expo, featuring thousands of toys. Held at the Central Culture Plaza, this year's event includes numerous famous toy manufacturers and retailers(零售商). Get ready to discover the latest global toy trends and make on-the-spot purchases* of your favorite toys!

The expo promises enjoyment for both adults and kids alike. Mark your calendars from August 19 to 23 and make sure you don't miss this incredible opportunity!

*Some of the invited artists' works are intended for exhibition purpose and not for sale.

From:	Jack Chen <jackchen87@geemail.com>
To:	inquiry@thetoyexpo.com
Subject:	Complaint about the Toy Expo

Dear organizer,

I am writing to share my mixed feelings about the Toy Expo. While I found the expo mostly satisfying, I was disappointed to learn that some of the toys were not available for purchase. It felt so bad that I could not buy the piece I fell in love with. Nevertheless, I must commend the expo for its variety of toys on display. As an adult without children, I am typically shy to enter a toy shop, but the expo provided a comfortable environment for me to explore and appreciate the wide selection of toys targeting adults. Therefore, I hope you will continue hosting this expo and address the problem I mentioned in the future.

Yours sincerely,
Jack Chen

26. What is true about the Toy Expo?
    A. It is held once a year.
    B. It is mainly for children to visit.
    C. Companies sell their old stock there.
    D. Toys exhibited in the expo are not for sale.

27. What aspect of the expo did Mr. Chen find satisfying?
    A. Its location and dates
    B. The possibility to buy toys
    C. Its toys for children to see
    D. The number of toys exhibited

28. In what part of the expo was Mr. Chen faced with a problem?
    A. In an artist's booth
    B. In a retailer's booth
    C. In a manufacturer's booth
    D. In a booth showing toy parts

Questions 29-31

Having trouble falling asleep at night? According to recent research, an estimated 237 million people worldwide suffer from insomnia (失眠). Insomnia can be caused by various factors, with emotional issues being the most common. Stress, anxiety, and depression are known to contribute to sleeplessness. Additionally, a family history of insomnia can increase the chance of experiencing similar symptoms. Your diet choices can also impact your sleep. Consuming too much alcohol or coffee can affect your sleep patterns, as can eating heavily late in the evening.

There are several strategies that can be helpful. The first and fundamental step is to establish a consistent sleep schedule. Maintain a regular bedtime and wake-up time, even on weekends. It is also a good idea to limit the use of electronic devices, including cell phones, before going to bed. These devices can keep the brain active and interfere with relaxation. Similarly, practicing meditation(冥想) before bedtime can promote a sense of peace, which is essential for a good night's sleep. These simple steps can significantly improve the quality of your sleep.

29. Which of the following is the best title for this article?
    A. The Latest Findings and New Facts about Insomnia
    B. Correcting Common Misunderstandings about Insomnia
    C. Effective Strategies for Improving Sleep Quality
    D. Why a Good Night's Sleep is Important for Your Health

30. According to this article, what is true about insomnia?
    A. It is essentially a psychological problem.
    B. One will suffer from insomnia if their parents do.
    C. Drinking wine can help us sleep better.
    D. Insomnia can be related to eating too much.

31. Which of the following is **NOT** a solution to insomnia?
    A. Avoiding drinking coffee
    B. Trying to go to bed and get up at fixed times
    C. Using a cell phone before sleep
    D. Meditating before going to bed

第 1 回
第 2 回
第 3 回
第 4 回
第 5 回
第 6 回
第 7 回
第 8 回
第 9 回
第 10 回

The leopard cat (石虎), a small wild cat species, is currently facing the threat of disappearing in Taiwan. Leopard cats are primarily found in Central Taiwan, particularly in Miaoli, Nantou, and Taichung. A study conducted in 2016 estimated the leopard cat population to be around 468-669 individuals. However, by 2022, the numbers had declined to 340-363.

Historically, leopard cats could be found throughout Taiwan. However, rapid economic development and population growth over the past 50 years have resulted in an alarming 80% decrease in the leopard cat population. One of the primary reasons for this decline is habitat (棲息地) loss due to land development. Human activities, such as exploiting natural lands in mountain areas, have intruded upon the habitats of leopard cats. As a result, they have experienced a reduction in genetic diversity (基因多樣性), leading to decreased breeding rates and weaker resistance to diseases.

The use of pesticides (殺蟲劑) and "roadkill" incidents also pose significant threats to the leopard cat population. While pesticides are applied to crops to combat pests, they can be consumed by mice, indirectly posing a threat to leopard cats as they rely on mice as a food source. Additionally, roadkill incidents, where wild animals are struck by vehicles, have emerged as a prominent factor contributing to the deaths of leopard cats. The fast-paced nature of driving in rural areas makes it difficult for drivers to react quickly and avoid hitting wildlife.

To address the situation faced by leopard cats, it is crucial to raise awareness about their endangered status. When there are more people informed and educated about the importance of protecting the species, it paves the way for greater support and more protective measures to be implemented.

32. What is this article mainly about?
    A. Recent studies on the leopard cat species
    B. The factors affecting the distribution of leopard cats
    C. The endangered situation of leopard cats
    D. The efforts to save leopard cats from disappearing

33. Based on the article, what is true about leopard cats?
    A. They are significantly decreasing in Taiwan.
    B. They can be found throughout Taiwan.
    C. They are often born with diseases.
    D. They can be poisoned by eating crops with pesticides.

34. According to the article, which of the following is **NOT** a factor threatening leopard cats?
    A. Land development
    B. Unlimited breeding
    C. Use of pesticides
    D. Vehicles on roads

35. What does the writer consider to be fundamental to saving leopard cats?
    A. Promoting tourism in mountain areas
    B. Fining careless drivers
    C. Raising people's awareness
    D. Implementing protective policies

TEST 08

GEPT 全民英檢

中級初試

題目本

本測驗分四部分，全為四選一之選擇題，共 35 題，作答時間約 30 分鐘。

第一部分：看圖辨義

共 5 題，試題冊上有數幅圖畫，每一圖畫有 1~3 個描述該圖的題目，每題請聽光碟放音機播出題目以及四個英語敘述之後，選出與所看到的圖畫最相符的答案，每題只播出一遍。

例：（看）

（聽）

Look at the picture. What is the woman doing?

A. She is looking at a sculpture.

B. She is appreciating a painting.

C. She is picking up a handbag.

D. She is entering a museum.

正確答案為 B。

聽力測驗第一部分自本頁開始。

A. Question 1

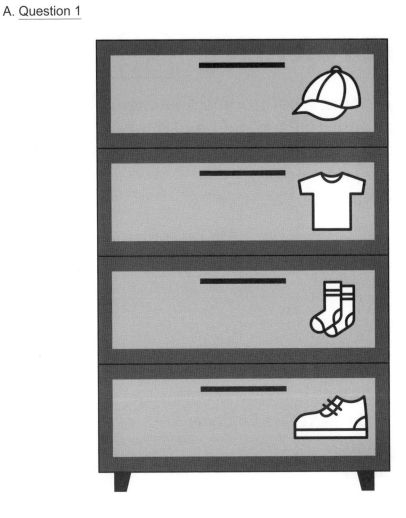

第1回

第2回

第3回

第4回

第5回

第6回

第7回

第8回

第9回

第10回

HOME FOR RENT

- 3 bedrooms, 2 bathrooms, 1 kitchen
- Near Kendrick Park and City Library
- $ 2,500 / month
- No pets, No smoking
- Date Available: Sat., July 7

 123-456-7890

WE'RE HIRING!

Job Title	Process Engineer
	Manufacturing
Requirements	• 1-year experience • Master's degree in engineering
Responsibilities	• Improve manufacturing process • Calculate and analyze equipment performance

第二部分：問答

共 10 題，每題請聽光碟放音機播出一英語問句或直述句之後，從試題冊上 A、B、C、D 四個回答或回應中，選出一個最適合者作答。每題只播出一遍。

例：（聽）Now that we've come to Kenting, we should try water sports.

（看）A. You can try harder next time.

B. Yes. I'm on the way there.

C. That sounds exciting to me.

D. We are coming in an hour.

正確答案為 C。

6. A. On Saturday or Sunday.

B. At least twice a month.

C. I often go by bicycle.

D. I sometimes go mountain climbing.

7. A. Yes, it should have opened now.

B. Because it is close to a mall.

C. A popular movie is released today.

D. They've changed their opening hours.

8. A. Have you tried having lunch there?

B. It'll be easy to meet the criteria.

C. Where can I find it, then?

D. I used to grab some food there.

9. A. Barbie organized the party.

B. Everyone in the Sales Department.

C. The party is on next Friday.

D. Jeremy likes to go to parties.

10. A. I forgot to load paper into the machine.

B. There isn't enough room to place it.

C. The supervisor hasn't approved it.

D. The copying machine is out-of-style.

11. A. I don't want to play music.
     B. Sorry, but my schedule is full.
     C. When will the first course be served?
     D. Yes, I can take it for granted.

12. A. It's not suitable for heavy items.
     B. I don't like traveling abroad.
     C. It's efficient for shipping goods.
     D. It's beneficial to the environment.

13. A. I've sent an email to them.
     B. We've been in contact for a year.
     C. I'll attend the meeting with her.
     D. I can't seem to find the menu.

14. A. I'm sorry for being late.
     B. It's really not your fault.
     C. How long do we have to wait?
     D. Where can we fly to instead?

15. A. You can come this Tuesday, then.
     B. Dr. Jones is currently on vacation.
     C. Sorry, we can't make it earlier.
     D. When would it be convenient for you?

第三部分：簡短對話

共 10 題，每題請聽光碟放音機播出一段對話及一個相關的問題後，從試題冊上 A、B、C、D 四個選項中選出一個最適合者作答。每段對話及問題只播出一遍。

例：（聽）（Woman） Excuse me. Does the next train go to the airport?

（Man）　　　No. Actually, this is the high speed rail station. You should go to the airport MRT station nearby to get to the airport.

（Woman） Thank you for letting me know. This is my first time taking a train to the airport, so I didn't notice that.

Question:　 What happened to the woman?

（看）A. She missed her train.
B. She got on the wrong train.
C. She went to the wrong station.
D. Her flight has already left.

正確答案為 C。

16. A. He was taking a shower.
B. He was having dinner.
C. He was in a meeting.
D. He left his phone at home.

17. A. Sunny but humid.
B. Cloudy and cold.
C. Chilly and rainy.
D. Rainy and windy.

18. A. She will sign up for it.
B. She has no interest in it.
C. She may not join it.
D. She wants to confirm its dates.

19. A. Make a phone call.
B. Send some information.
C. Prepare a presentation.
D. Contact Stella.

20. A. Tomorrow.
B. This Wednesday.
C. This Thursday.
D. Next Monday.

21. A. She does not know their location.
B. There is a supply shortage.
C. The store does not sell eggs.
D. She did not call to reserve eggs.

22. A. To retrieve a lost item.
    B. To make an appointment.
    C. To order some clothes.
    D. To ask about business hours.

23. A. She looks attractive.
    B. She seldom talks to others.
    C. She loves to chat with people.
    D. Her grades are very good.

24. **Today's Appointments**

Patient Name	Time	Treatment
Ms. Johnson	1:00 p.m.	Checkup
Mr. Norwood	1:30 p.m.	Teeth cleaning
Ms. Tanner	2:20 p.m.	Checkup
Mr. Hoffman	3:00 p.m.	Teeth cleaning

   A. Ms. Johnson.
   B. Mr. Norwood.
   C. Ms. Tanner.
   D. Mr. Hoffman.

25.

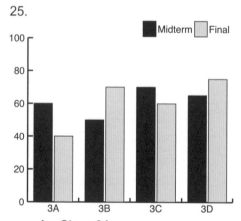

   A. Class 3A.
   B. Class 3B.
   C. Class 3C.
   D. Class 3D.

第四部分：簡短談話

共 10 題，每題請聽光碟放音機播出一段談話及一個相關的問題後，從試題冊上 A、B、C、D 四個選項中選出一個最適合者作答。每段談話及問題只播出一遍。

例：（聽）Teenagers can easily feel hurt in their social lives. When they have difficulty making friends, they may feel worried about going to school. Even if they are popular at school, they may be persuaded to do things they don't like, such as smoking or drinking, under peer pressure. The stress of fitting in can eventually make them mentally ill.

Question: According to the speaker, what makes a teenager try smoking even though they are not interested?

（看）A. Parents' complaint.
B. Friends' persuasion.
C. Romantic relationship.
D. Academic pressure.

正確答案為 B。

26. A. The owner didn't learn cooking.
B. Its food did not taste good.
C. Food portions were not satisfying.
D. It was not advertised on TV.

27. A. Oral practice.
B. English writing.
C. Listening to the radio.
D. Studying past questions.

28. A. It will be sunny.
B. There will only be a few clouds.
C. It could possibly rain.
D. A storm will arrive.

29. A. It contains fried eggs.
B. Its filling is seasoned.
C. It is made using fresh white bread.
D. It is more convenient not to cut it.

30. A. To exchange a product.
B. To get his money back.
C. To confirm a delivery.
D. To place an order.

31. A. Hire a cleaning specialist.
    B. Watch some videos.
    C. Get some benefits.
    D. Purchase its products.

32. A. The session will begin at noon.
    B. The schedule has been changed.
    C. Everyone should attend on April 23.
    D. There is an alternative date.

33. A. She just got a promotion.
    B. She just changed jobs.
    C. She has won an advertising award.
    D. She has been a salesperson.

34.

Model	Facial Recognition	Screen Size	Weight	Battery Life
F20	✓	6.7 inches	240g	22 hours
F10	✓	6.1 inches	200g	20 hours
S500	✕	6.1 inches	175g	25 hours
S300	✕	5.5 inches	140g	23 hours

    A. F20.
    B. F10.
    C. S500.
    D. S300.

35.

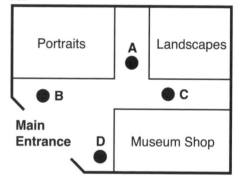

    A. Spot A.
    B. Spot B.
    C. Spot C.
    D. Spot D.

本測驗分三部分，全為四選一之選擇題，共 35 題，作答時間 45 分鐘。

第一部分：詞彙

共 10 題，每題含一個空格。請由試題冊上的四個選項中選出最適合題意的字或詞作答。

1. Terry _____ the success of this project, but the idea actually came from Jessica.
   - A. brought up
   - B. tucked in
   - C. took credit for
   - D. dropped out of

2. Jane headed to the kitchen _____ when her mom told her to stop playing games and do the dishes.
   - A. reluctantly
   - B. remotely
   - C. remarkably
   - D. relatively

3. Sally has strong determination in everything. Once she has made up her mind, she will _____ herself to a task until the end.
   - A. resign
   - B. devote
   - C. educate
   - D. surrender

4. The exchange student from Japan is trying his best to overcome the language _____ in order to adapt to life in France.
   - A. abuse
   - B. barrier
   - C. clash
   - D. decay

5. The maximum _____ of this elevator is 500 kilograms or 8 adults, and it would be unsafe to exceed this limit.
   - A. consideration
   - B. coincidence
   - C. capability
   - D. capacity

6. People who are color-blind cannot make a _____ between certain colors.
   A. prediction
   B. distinction
   C. conclusion
   D. reservation

7. The electricity _____ by the new power plant is expected to meet the daily need of 2000 households.
   A. registered
   B. withdrawn
   C. generated
   D. overthrown

8. The government's policies aimed at promoting industrial development have led to a significant increase of new _____ facilities.
   A. recreation
   B. educational
   C. commercial
   D. manufacturing

9. With this e-banking app, you can easily check your account balance and investment performance _____.
   A. on the rise
   B. on short notice
   C. at all costs
   D. at a glance

10. _____ materials should not be stored near sources of heat or open flames.
    A. aggressive
    B. defensive
    C. explosive
    D. offensive

第二部分：段落填空

共 10 題，包括二個段落，每個段落各含 5 個空格。請由試題冊上四個選項中選出最適合題意的字或詞作答。

Questions 11-15

　　With real-name social media sites such as Facebook, it is now easy to find a friend we have ___(11)___ with for a long time. However, this kind of sites may also be used as a tool for "doxing". Doxing means finding and spreading private information about someone online, such as their name and address, usually ___(12)___ as a kind of punishment or revenge. For example, when someone posts an opinion on a controversial (爭議性的) topic, those who disagree may try to find out the person's real name or even workplace on social media sites. By revealing the person's ___(13)___, they may attract more people to harass him or her, both online and in real life. The ___(14)___ may feel unsafe or frightened, and their relationships and professional reputation may be negatively affected. Even though social media sites ___(15)___, such convenience can also be abused to invade someone's privacy.

11.　A.　lost contact
　　　B.　caught up
　　　C.　closed a deal
　　　D.　come to terms

12.　A.　intended
　　　B.　provided
　　　C.　qualified
　　　D.　specified

13.　A.　reality
　　　B.　identity
　　　C.　property
　　　D.　personality

14.　A.　victim
　　　B.　civilian
　　　C.　refugee
　　　D.　spectator

15.　A.　allow people to share their thoughts
　　　B.　make it easy to improve our social connections
　　　C.　have changed the way we consume information
　　　D.　can be used by businesses to reach their customers

Questions 16-20

Emotional eating ___(16)___ the behavior of using food to cope with negative emotions or stress. The reasons behind such behavior are mostly ___(17)___ the difficulty in managing one's emotions. When we are emotionally troubled, we may see eating things as a way to comfort ourselves and stop giving attention to our bad feelings. ___(18)___ . For example, anxiety, ___(19)___ in relationships, and shame about size or weight, can all contribute to our mood decline. Even though eating may relieve our stress for a while in such a situation, it cannot solve the problem itself. What is worse, if we do not feel comforted enough, we may continue eating in an attempt to find relief, which can lead to overeating and cause more self-blame and guilt. Therefore, we should ___(20)___ and deal with our emotional problem instead of trying to forget about it by eating.

16. A. takes up
     B. refers to
     C. makes up for
     D. works out

17. A. covered with
     B. compared with
     C. related to
     D. subject to

18. A. They can also have some positive effects
     B. Many people turn to food for stress relief
     C. Such feelings can be caused by various reasons
     D. Some find it helpful for cheering themselves up

19. A. achievement
     B. commitment
     C. disappointment
     D. encouragement

20. A. criticize
     B. memorize
     C. recognize
     D. sympathize

第三部分：閱讀理解

共 15 題，包括數篇短文，每篇短文後有 2~4 個相關問題。請由試題冊上四個選項中選出最適合者作答。

Questions 21-22

Summer Heaven
Special Offer
July 1 – August 31
Our only sale of the year

The water is calling, and the swimsuit season is nearly upon us, making now the perfect time to add some new swimsuits to your wardrobe!

Summer Heaven is delighted to offer special discounts for all customers. A huge selection of bikinis, swim dresses, one-pieces, and more are now available. Take this chance to purchase all kinds of swimwear at much lower prices!

*Discounts are offered both online and offline. To check our discounted items, visit us at 709C Sunshine Road or shop online at summerheavenltd.com.

---

21. What is the main purpose of this advertisement?
    A. To launch a new product line
    B. To announce a sales campaign
    C. To advertise a new swimwear shop
    D. To offer gifts to selected customers

22. What is indicated about the discounts?
    A. They are prepared for returning customers.
    B. They only apply to Internet shopping.
    C. They are only available for two months.
    D. They will be given again later this year.

第 1 回
第 2 回
第 3 回
第 4 回
第 5 回
第 6 回
第 7 回
第 8 回
第 9 回
第 10 回

From:	Richard Sanchez <ricsaz@geemail.com>
To:	Jenna Lawton <jenltt@coldmail.com>
Subject:	Meeting on February 13th

Dear Ms. Lawton,

On behalf of Gerald Catering(外燴服務), I would like to thank you for choosing to collaborate with us. We look forward to sharing our food and services with you and your guests.

I am writing to double-check your order for your meeting on February 13th. You've ordered 13 chicken barbecues, 15 buttered vegetables, and 10 seafood pastas. If there are any changes, please let me know.

As to the drinks, for your group of twenty people, I recommend our special drinks package, which is currently offered at a discounted price. We have a variety of coffees, juices, teas, and sodas to choose from. You can check the menu on our website. Please confirm the final details of your selection by January 20th.

You can also check for our other offers and discounts on our website at www. geraldcatering.com. Thank you again for choosing Gerald Catering for your catering needs.

Richard Sanchez
Event Coordinator, Gerald Catering

23. What is the purpose of this e-mail?
    A. To schedule an event
    B. To promote a new event
    C. To confirm some information
    D. To offer a discount on delivery

24. How many people are expected to attend the meeting?
    A. 10
    B. 13
    C. 15
    D. 20

25. What is Ms. Lawton asked to do?
    A. Sign up at the website
    B. Select some kinds of drinks
    C. Visit the physical store next time
    D. Confirm attendance at the meeting

Questions 26-28 are based on information provided in the following flyer and email.

Taysom's Kitchen

CLASS	TEACHER
Delicious Kimchi Stew (August 8, 2:00 – 4:30 p.m.)	Jason Lee
Classical French Cooking (August 12, 6:00 – 8:30 p.m.)	Anthony Brooks
Hands-on Pizza (August 23, 2:30 – 4:00 p.m.)	Marco Rossi

Are you interested in learning how to cook, but don't know where to begin? Our excellent teachers provide easy-to-understand methods and techniques for you to create delicious dishes. In our classes, you'll also learn about nutrition, food safety, and ways to save money on your groceries. After each class, participants will receive a bag of ingredients for them to re-create the dishes they've learned to make. Choose a class you're drawn to and sign up today!

To sign up, call 376-000-0000 or visit taysomskitchen.com

From:	Laura Parkinson <laupn27@mail.ndusa.com>
To:	Elizabeth Schultz <elibshz@mailgun.org>
Subject:	Taysom's Kitchen's cooking class

Dear Ms. Schultz,

The class you signed up for has been rescheduled because the Italian food teacher has to attend to an urgent matter on the original date. The new date will be August 30, and the time and location remain the same. If you are unable to attend, please call us to arrange for your money back. Thank you for your understanding.

Yours sincerely,
Laura Parkinson
Taysom's Kitchen

26. What is **NOT** a benefit of taking a class at Taysom's Kitchen?
    A. Acquiring more knowledge about food
    B. Knowing about the latest diet trends
    C. Learning how to be economical
    D. Receiving some groceries for cooking

27. Which class did Ms. Schultz sign up for?
    A. Delicious Kimchi Stew
    B. Classical French Cooking
    C. Hands-on Pizza
    D. She has not signed up for a class yet.

28. What is true about the rescheduled class?
    A. It will be taught by another Italian food teacher.
    B. It will be earlier than originally scheduled.
    C. It will be held at a different place.
    D. It allows students to cancel their registrations.

第 1 回
第 2 回
第 3 回
第 4 回
第 5 回
第 6 回
第 7 回
第 8 回
第 9 回
第 10 回

Questions 29-31

The Ebola virus was first discovered in 1976, in Congo and Sudan. The main targets of Ebola virus infection are humans and primates(靈長類動物) such as monkeys. Currently, it is believed that fruit bats are the natural host of the Ebola virus.

Ebola can spread through contact with body fluids of an infected person or dead patient. Studies have shown that the Ebola virus cannot be transmitted through water or mosquito bites, and there has been no case report of spreading through air.

Once infected, the patient will have some symptoms, including sudden high fever, head and muscle aches, followed by vomiting, diarrhea(腹瀉), and internal and external bleeding. In severe cases, liver damage, kidney failure, shock, and multiple organ failure may occur. Therefore, there is a high chance that an Ebola patient may die.

Unfortunately, there is not a totally effective cure for the Ebola virus yet, and most of the time the only help a doctor can give is to ensure patients take in enough water and keep them isolated from others.

29. What is true about Ebola virus infection?
    A. It only affects human beings.
    B. It is not possible through touching a dead patient.
    C. It is very possible that one dies after being infected.
    D. There is not any medicine used for treating it.

30. What is a possible way of being infected with Ebola?
    A. Drinking water that is not clean
    B. Being bitten by a mosquito
    C. Talking with a patient
    D. Touching the blood of a patient

31. What does the author imply in the last paragraph?
    A. It is possible to wipe out the disease by supplying sufficient medicine.
    B. People can prevent the disease by getting a vaccine.
    C. Drinking water does not help patients to maintain their condition.
    D. Patients should be treated in separate rooms.

第1回
第2回
第3回
第4回
第5回
第6回
第7回
第8回
第9回
第10回

Questions 32-35

　　While many organizations provide meals and clothes to homeless(無家的) people, those in need often have little say in what they receive. However, The Street Store, an initiative(倡議) founded by an advertising agency in Cape Town, offers a different approach to helping those without shelter.

　　The Street Store aims to change the situation that homeless people rarely have the opportunity to choose what they want. Instead of distributing used clothes to those in need in a top-down manner, it encourages people to gather donated clothes and open a "pop-up store on the street". Even though it is called a store, its "customers", namely the homeless, will not be charged. By allowing the homeless to choose the items they need in a way like shopping, such a "store" gives them a greater sense of dignity.

　　With some donated clothes and a street location, anyone in the world can host a street store in their local community. The Street Store provides a guidebook showing how to host such an event, as well as posters and other materials that can be printed out and displayed at the store. By 2023, there has been 1,000 events hosted, benefitting over a million people around the world.

　　Besides the design of the street store events, the attitude of volunteers also plays a role in making them so successful. They treat everyone with kindness regardless of their circumstances. For the homeless visiting the stores, the emotional support they receive from the volunteers is just as valuable as the clothes they get.

32. What does a "street store" do?
    A. Selling second-hand clothes
    B. Distributing donated clothes to those in need
    C. Displaying clothes for the homeless to choose from
    D. Donating to the homeless on the street

33. What is true about The Street Store?
    A. It is a global organization.
    B. It is a project of an advertising company.
    C. It gathers donated clothes.
    D. It has hosted 1,000 events by itself.

34. What does one need to do before hosting a street store event?
    A. Prepare a collection of donated clothes
    B. Design some posters to be displayed
    C. Rent a shop space in a building
    D. Hire some cashiers

35. What does the author want to stress in the last paragraph?
    A. The attitude of volunteers is enough to make a street store event
       successful.
    B. The volunteers treat the homeless nicely out of pity for them.
    C. The clothes given to the homeless contribute to their emotional well-being.
    D. The homeless need not only material but also emotional care.

第 1 回
第 2 回
第 3 回
第 4 回
第 5 回
第 6 回
第 7 回
第 8 回
第 9 回
第 10 回

TEST 09

GEPT
全民英檢

中級初試

題目本

本測驗分四部分，全為四選一之選擇題，共 35 題，作答時間約 30 分鐘。

第一部分：看圖辨義

共 5 題，試題冊上有數幅圖畫，每一圖畫有 1~3 個描述該圖的題目，每題請聽光碟放音機播出題目以及四個英語敘述之後，選出與所看到的圖畫最相符的答案，每題只播出一遍。

例：（看）

（聽）

Look at the picture. What is the woman doing?

A. She is looking at a sculpture.

B. She is appreciating a painting.

C. She is picking up a handbag.

D. She is entering a museum.

正確答案為 B。

A. <u>Question 1</u>

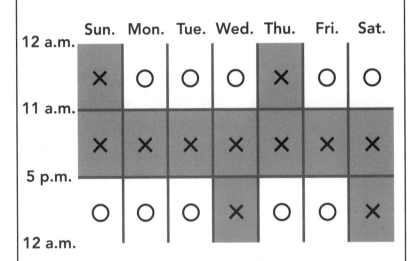

Rose Apartment
Food Waste Collection Spot

	Sun.	Mon.	Tue.	Wed.	Thu.	Fri.	Sat.
12 a.m. – 11 a.m.	✕	◯	◯	◯	✕	◯	◯
11 a.m. – 5 p.m.	✕	✕	✕	✕	✕	✕	✕
5 p.m. – 12 a.m.	◯	◯	◯	✕	◯	◯	✕

- Leave food waste here only during time slots marked "◯".
- Hard materials, such as bones and coconut shells, are not accepted.

B. Questions 2 and 3

TRICK OR TREAT!

YOU ARE INVITED TO A
Halloween Costume Party

SUNDAY, 30 OCTOBER | 7-11 *p.m.*
Free Entry

Wear you scariest costume at
The Pitts
and get a chance to win a prize!

C. Questions 4 and 5

To-Do List

☑ Shop for groceries

☐ Mend the hole in John's pants

☑ Go to the handcraft class

☐ Clean the kitchen and bathroom

☐ Pick up the kids after school

第二部分：問答

共 10 題，每題請聽光碟放音機播出一英語問句或直述句之後，從試題冊上 A、B、C、D 四個回答或回應中，選出一個最適合者作答。每題只播出一遍。

例： （聽）Now that we've come to Kenting, we should try water sports.
   （看）A. You can try harder next time.
        B. Yes. I'm on the way there.
        C. That sounds exciting to me.
        D. We are coming in an hour.

正確答案為 C。

6. A. Who will handle her duties?
   B. I've never been there either.
   C. Oh, really? How was her trip?
   D. She is good at speaking Japanese.

7. A. It's been broken since last Saturday.
   B. It's very quiet when turned on.
   C. Is it too cold in the room?
   D. I can't stand the hot weather, either.

8. A. I don't go camping very often.
   B. Rain or shine, we will be there.
   C. We could see the stars in the sky.
   D. It was like a candle in the wind.

9. A. I usually go to bed early.
   B. I watched a TV series until four.
   C. Actually, I didn't have anything.
   D. Do I look like a lazy person?

10. A. The train was a bit delayed.
    B. I'm sorry, but it's not the case.
    C. I don't see what you mean.
    D. I can't seem to find my passport.

第 1 回
第 2 回
第 3 回
第 4 回
第 5 回
第 6 回
第 7 回
第 8 回
第 9 回
第 10 回

11. A. I'm afraid of deep water.
     B. I don't like changes.
     C. How much each time?
     D. Can you imagine how?

12. A. It's on last Saturday.
     B. It feels wonderful being married.
     C. We spent $200 on it.
     D. We had a date at a café.

13. A. She's so brave to come here by herself.
     B. Let's take her to the information desk.
     C. My daughter's wearing a pink dress, though.
     D. It's no use being a cry baby.

14. A. I've spent a lot on the purse.
     B. I already have one similar to it.
     C. I had to settle for the second best.
     D. I needed to exchange it for another one.

15. A. He must have missed a lot of scenes.
     B. I love going to the movies, too.
     C. It's never too late to apologize.
     D. What can we do to help him?

第三部分：簡短對話

共 10 題，每題請聽光碟放音機播出一段對話及一個相關的問題後，從試題冊上 A、B、C、D 四個選項中選出一個最適合者作答。每段對話及問題只播出一遍。

例：　（聽）　（Woman） Excuse me. Does the next train go to the airport?

　　　　　　（Man）　　No. Actually, this is the high speed rail station. You should go to the airport MRT station nearby to get to the airport.

　　　　　　（Woman） Thank you for letting me know. This is my first time taking a train to the airport, so I didn't notice that.

　　　　　　Question:　　What happened to the woman?

　　（看）　A. She missed her train.

　　　　　　B. She got on the wrong train.

　　　　　　C. She went to the wrong station.

　　　　　　D. Her flight has already left.

正確答案為 C。

16. A. Watching TV.
    B. Reading a novel.
    C. Investigating a case.
    D. Making a police report.

17. A. He canceled it.
    B. It arrived too late.
    C. It was not prepared at all.
    D. It was delivered to the wrong place.

18. A. He is sick.
    B. He did not do his homework.
    C. He is not good at math.
    D. He did not sleep well last night.

19. A. At a historic site.
    B. At an art school.
    C. At a gallery.
    D. At a trading company.

20. A. Its freshness.
    B. Its flavor.
    C. Its price.
    D. Its portion size.

21. A. It will not arrive immediately.
    B. It does not come very often.
    C. It does not stop at Citizen Park.
    D. Its stop is far from their destination.

第1回
第2回
第3回
第4回
第5回
第6回
第7回
第8回
第9回
第10回

22. A. It is raining outside.
    B. It is not waterproof.
    C. Her water bottle is not closed well.
    D. Her water bottle is squeezed in it.

23. A. Eat out.
    B. Clean up.
    C. Cook dinner.
    D. Have a party.

24.

✈ Departures			
Time	Destination	Flight	Remarks
09:00	San Francisco	GU148	Canceled
09:20	San Francisco	TA1107	Canceled
09:50	Los Angeles	GU256	On Time
10:10	Los Angeles	TA2046	On Time

    A. GU148.
    B. TA1107.
    C. GU256.
    D. TA2046.

25.

Edith Yoga School
July

Yin Yoga
All levels / become more flexible and energetic

Power Yoga
Intermediate / challenge your strength and endurance

Restorative Yoga
All levels / relax deeply and reduce your stress

Pilates
Intermediate / strengthen your core and be more flexible

Call 000-0000 for more information

    A. Yin yoga.
    B. Power yoga.
    C. Restorative yoga.
    D. Pilates.

第四部分：簡短談話

共 10 題，每題請聽光碟放音機播出一段談話及一個相關的問題後，從試題冊上 A、B、C、D 四個選項中選出一個最適合者作答。每段談話及問題只播出一遍。

例：（聽）Teenagers can easily feel hurt in their social lives. When they have difficulty making friends, they may feel worried about going to school. Even if they are popular at school, they may be persuaded to do things they don't like, such as smoking or drinking, under peer pressure. The stress of fitting in can eventually make them mentally ill.

Question: According to the speaker, what makes a teenager try smoking even though they are not interested?

（看）A. Parents' complaint.
B. Friends' persuasion.
C. Romantic relationship.
D. Academic pressure.

正確答案為 B。

26. A. She forgot her daughter's birthday.
B. She was on a business trip.
C. She was busy working on a project.
D. She got a promotion then.

27. A. He was walking too fast.
B. He entered the dog's space.
C. He was too careful.
D. He woke up the dog.

28. A. Off-season clothes.
B. Coats.
C. Sweaters.
D. T-shirts.

29. A. They went to different high schools.
B. She refused to see Kelly.
C. She argued with Kelly in a café.
D. There was a misunderstanding.

30. A. Activity tracking.
B. Health monitoring.
C. Mobile communication.
D. Travel planning.

第 1 回
第 2 回
第 3 回
第 4 回
第 5 回
第 6 回
第 7 回
第 8 回
第 9 回
第 10 回

31. A. The speaker's co-worker.
    B. The speaker's landlord.
    C. The speaker's aunt.
    D. The speaker's roommate.

32. A. Checking class schedules.
    B. Ordering some products.
    C. Leaving a message.
    D. Signing up for a class.

33. A. He did not want to prepare
       dinner.
    B. He did not like the speaker's
       cooking.
    C. He wanted the speaker to take
       a rest.
    D. He forgot the speaker's
       birthday.

34.

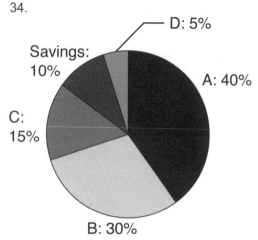

A. Sector A.
B. Sector B.
C. Sector C.
D. Sector D.

35.

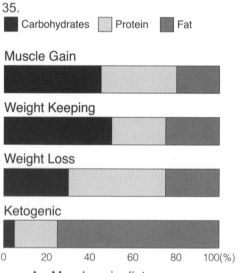

A. Muscle gain diet.
B. Weight keeping diet.
C. Weight loss diet.
D. Ketogenic diet.

本測驗分三部分,全為四選一之選擇題,共 35 題,作答時間 45 分鐘。

第一部分:詞彙

共 10 題,每題含一個空格。請由試題冊上的四個選項中選出最適合題意的字或詞作答。

1. All of the classmates were invited, but only a _____ of them attended Sally's birthday party.
    A. crowd
    B. handful
    C. bundle
    D. quantity

2. Marching bands and colorful floats with performers filled the streets during the annual summer _____.
    A. parade
    B. concert
    C. convention
    D. demonstration

3. Some consider that _____ power plants are not safe because they could release dangerous levels of radiation in the event of an accident.
    A. solar
    B. nuclear
    C. efficient
    D. industrial

4. Although the twins look _____, their personalities are complete opposites.
    A. imaginative
    B. ignorant
    C. ironic
    D. identical

5. Since Aaron _____ to become a doctor, he has been showing great passion for his chosen path by reading medical textbooks every day.
    A. stood in others' shoes
    B. called it off
    C. made up his mind
    D. lost his head

第 1 回
第 2 回
第 3 回
第 4 回
第 5 回
第 6 回
第 7 回
第 8 回
第 9 回
第 10 回

6. After spending hours _____ the criminal, the police finally caught him in an abandoned garage.
   A. pursuing   B. investigating
   C. searching   D. charging

7. Due to frequent power failures, the factory could not _____ goods efficiently, resulting in production delays and financial losses.
   A. accommodate   B. manufacture
   C. distinguish   D. stimulate

8. Several _____ ago, when mobile phones were not yet common, people relied on telephones and face-to-face communication to exchange information.
   A. ages   B. quarters
   C. centuries   D. decades

9. The weather in summer afternoons _____ take a turn for the worse, so I always carry an umbrella with me just in case it starts raining.
   A. used to   B. tends to
   C. intends to   D. cannot but

10. Just a small amount of _____ can negatively affect your judgment and physical control while driving.
    A. alcohol   B. carbon
    C. fragrance   D. moisture

第二部分：段落填空

共 10 題，包括二個段落，每個段落各含 5 個空格。請由試題冊上四個選項中選出最適合題意的字或詞作答。

Questions 11-15

Eros, the Greek God of love, possessed the power to blind people with his control over their ___(11)___ . When struck by Eros' golden arrow, people would deeply fall in love. ___(12)___ , those hit by lead arrows would become uninterested in love.

One day, when Apollo claimed that he was superior, Eros was offended and shot Apollo with a golden arrow. Instantly, Apollo fell in love with a passing nymph(仙女) named Daphne, who was ___(13)___ struck by a lead arrow and swiftly fled. After a long chase, Daphne became ___(14)___ and unable to run any further, so she prayed to her father Peneus to be transformed into a laurel(月桂) tree.

___(15)___ , Apollo's love remained the same. Amazingly, the laurel tree retains green leaves around the year since then.

11. A. affections
    B. communications
    C. expectations
    D. imaginations

12. A. Conversely
    B. Dramatically
    C. Suspiciously
    D. Unexpectedly

13. A. later on
    B. in particular
    C. for the moment
    D. as a result

14. A. concentrated
    B. determined
    C. exhausted
    D. frustrated

15. A. Contrary to popular belief
    B. Because of his continuous effort
    C. Surprised by such a sudden change
    D. Despite witnessing this transformation

第 1 回
第 2 回
第 3 回
第 4 回
第 5 回
第 6 回
第 7 回
第 8 回
第 9 回
第 10 回

Questions 16-20

Imprinting(銘印現象) is a learning behavior commonly observed in animals such as birds, chickens, geese, and ducks. It involves young animals __(16)__ the first moving object they see after birth, typically their parents. __(17)__, baby ducks are well-known for being sensitive to imprinting. Once a duck __(18)__ from its egg, it recognizes and imitates anything it sees in its immediate environment, considering the first moving object it encounters __(19)__ its mother. __(20)__ the object has certain characteristics, it can make imprinting happen, even if it is a human being.

16. A. being easily confused by
    B. showing curiosity toward
    C. becoming overly cautious about
    D. developing a conscious connection to

17. A. At first
    B. However
    C. Fortunately
    D. For example

18. A. escapes
    B. hatches
    C. launches
    D. vanishes

19. A. for
    B. as
    C. with
    D. in

20. A. If only
    B. As long as
    C. By the time
    D. In order that

第三部分：閱讀理解

共 15 題，包括數篇短文，每篇短文後有 2~4 個相關問題。請由試題冊上四個選項
中選出最適合者作答。

Questions 21-22

Umbrella that lights up rainy days

Japanese company Mabu grabs attention with their innovative "Umbrella Lantern". By equipping a conventional umbrella with LED lights, they create a lantern-like device, lighting up the surroundings in the dark. This eye-catching invention not only looks unique but also ensures its users' safety when they walk in the night by making them more visible to car drivers.

---

21. What kind of product is introduced in this article?
    A. An umbrella with an added feature
    B. A lantern in the shape of an umbrella
    C. An improved type of LED light
    D. A fashion item gaining popularity

22. According to the article, what is true about the product?
    A. It is only available in Japan.
    B. It looks more like a lantern than an umbrella.
    C. It grabs attention from the fashion industry.
    D. It can help prevent car accidents.

第 1 回
第 2 回
第 3 回
第 4 回
第 5 回
第 6 回
第 7 回
第 8 回
第 9 回
第 10 回

Dear Winnie,

    I am so happy to invite you to be part of the most significant day for Kevin and me. You have been a valuable friend since our elementary school days. When I was down because of not getting into my first-choice college, you were there to encourage me and tell me to never give up on my dreams. That was why I started to learn graphic design and eventually established my current business. I also appreciate that you helped me build a client base so I can help many companies promote their products and services.

    In addition to all of this, of course, what I appreciate the most is that you introduced me to your cousin, Kevin, after my painful breakup. Kevin and I have found love together, and now we are beginning a new chapter of our lives. Your role in bringing us together is truly priceless, so I would be absolutely delighted if you could join us and be part of this special occasion. Please save the date!

With warmest regards,
Lesley

23. What kind of occasion is Lesley most likely inviting Winnie to?
    A. A wedding
    B. An anniversary
    C. An award ceremony
    D. An opening ceremony

24. What kind of business does Lesley own?
    A. A talent agency
    B. An advertising agency
    C. A real estate company
    D. A manufacturing company

25. According to the letter, what is true about Kevin?
    A. He is a business partner of Lesley.
    B. He is breaking up with Lesley.
    C. He is Lesley's relative.
    D. He was introduced to Lesley by Winnie.

第 1 回
第 2 回
第 3 回
第 4 回
第 5 回
第 6 回
第 7 回
第 8 回
第 9 回
第 10 回

Questions 26-28 are based on information provided in the following advertisement and email.

Join Our Santa Claus Team!

Are you filled with holiday spirit and ready to spread joy and cheer? Join us to play Santa at Marcy Department Store! You will have the opportunity to engage with children and families, making their holiday season extra special.

Date: December 19-25 (choose your preferred duty days)
Time: 12 p.m. – 10 p.m. (daily)
Location: Marcy Department Store
Pay: $150 per day

Requirements:
- Warm and friendly manner
- Ability to engage and interact with children of all ages
- Comfortable wearing the Santa Claus costume
- Availability for full-day commitment

To express your interest, please contact us at recruit@marcydepstore.com.

From:	nicholas_barry@sanatmail.com
To:	recruit@marcydepstore.com
Subject:	Santa Claus Team Application

Dear Hiring Manager,

I am writing to express my interest in joining the Santa Claus Team at Marcy Department Store for the upcoming holiday season. During my previous experience working with children in a preschool, I have demonstrated the ability to capture the attention and interest of children. I think it is because children are naturally drawn to my welcoming personality. Moreover, I have had the opportunity to play characters there once in a while by wearing costumes, making me well-suited for the role of Santa Claus.

I am available every afternoon until six from December 19 to 25. Should you require any additional information or need to discuss my application further, please feel free to reach out to me at your convenience.

Regards,
Nicholas Barry

26. What is the purpose of the advertisement?
    A. To hire a full-time employee
    B. To fill a temporary job opening
    C. To promote a Christmas sales event
    D. To advertise a role-playing competition

27. What kind of work did Mr. Barry most likely do before?
    A. A nurse
    B. An actor
    C. A teacher
    D. A street artist

28. What aspect of Mr. Barry might be the reason that he would not be considered?
    A. His personality
    B. His interaction with children
    C. His previous experience
    D. His available hours

第1回
第2回
第3回
第4回
第5回
第6回
第7回
第8回
第9回
第10回

Sometimes, finding a balance between environmental friendliness and ensuring people's health can be challenging. An example of this challenge is evident in the date labels found on food packages. In the past, food packages usually had a "use by" label, indicating that the food would spoil and be no longer suitable for consumption after that date. Nowadays, however, it is more common to encounter the "best before" label instead. "Best before" indicates an earlier date compared to "use by", suggesting that the food may lose its peak freshness after the specific date, rather than become unsafe for consumption.

Some environment activists(積極分子) argue that the shift to "best before" has led to a rise in food waste because most people do not correctly understand its meaning. When a food product is past its "best before" date, people would take it as spoiled and throw it away instead of consume it while it is still edible. **Ironically**, manufacturers might be satisfied with such a situation, as the demand for their products might increase because of the waste, resulting in higher profits.

In an effort to address this issue, the Food and Drug Administration (FDA) has recommended the use of two distinct labels: "best if used by" for indicating freshness and "use by" for products that tend to spoil. This approach aims to provide labels that consumers can easily understand and interpret.

29. According to this article, which of the following descriptions is true?
    A. The FDA suggests that all food products be labeled with "use by".
    B. In the past, most food products were labeled with "best before".
    C. Food products were considered still edible after the "use by" date.
    D. Most people think that food products spoil after the "best before" date.

30. Which of the following is closest in meaning to the word "**Ironically**" in the 2nd paragraph?
    A. Ideally
    B. Strangely
    C. Famously
    D. Particularly

31. Why are manufacturers of food products satisfied with the situation that "best before" is misunderstood?
    A. Consumers will buy more of their products.
    B. They can sell their products at higher prices.
    C. They are allowed to pay less tax to the government.
    D. They can be more environmentally friendly by reducing waste.

32. What does "best if used by" mean?
    A. Freshest if consumed before
    B. Retaining more nutrition before
    C. Less healthy after
    D. Not suitable for consumption after

第1回
第2回
第3回
第4回
第5回
第6回
第7回
第8回
第9回
第10回

Questions 33-35

The concept of the "four-day workweek" is currently a subject of intense debate. It refers to the idea of reducing the workweek to four days while preserving productivity and salary levels at the same time. The concept already existed several decades ago, yet it was during the COVID-19 pandemic that it gained widespread attention. As organizations adapted to remote work arrangements, people started to question traditional work structures and consider the possibility of enhancing work-life balance by reducing workdays.

Despite the growing interest in the four-day workweek, it is worth noting that not every worker supports this work pattern. According to research, while 92% of workers are open to the idea of a four-day workweek, 55% are concerned about potentially causing negative response from customers or partners. Additionally, 46% of workers are worried about that four-day workweek might impact on company profits, and a significant 73% of workers fear that it could lead to longer working hours per day.

Even though the four-day workweek has only been experimented with on a limited scale in a few countries, such as Ireland, Canada, and the UK, it is expected to be adopted by more organizations as its advantages become evident in the near future.

33. What is this article mainly about?
    A. The effect of the pandemic on work structures
    B. How remote work helps improve work-life balance
    C. A growing trend of reducing workdays
    D. The concerns surrounding a new idea of working

34. Which of the following is **NOT** true about the "four-day workweek"?
    A. No country has made it a requirement yet.
    B. Salary will be reduced under this work pattern.
    C. It creates more days of rest for workers.
    D. Ideally, it will not make workers less productive.

35. According to the article, which of the following raises the highest level of
    concern among workers?
    A. They might need to work for more hours a day.
    B. Customers and partners might not be satisfied.
    C. Companies' profits might decrease.
    D. People are not ready to accept the new idea.

第 1 回
第 2 回
第 3 回
第 4 回
第 5 回
第 6 回
第 7 回
第 8 回
第 9 回
第 10 回

TEST 10

GEPT
全民英檢
中級初試

題目本

本測驗分四部分，全為四選一之選擇題，共 35 題，作答時間約 30 分鐘。

第一部分：看圖辨義

共 5 題，試題冊上有數幅圖畫，每一圖畫有 1~3 個描述該圖的題目，每題請聽光碟放音機播出題目以及四個英語敘述之後，選出與所看到的圖畫最相符的答案，每題只播出一遍。

例：（看）

（聽）

Look at the picture. What is the woman doing?

A. She is looking at a sculpture.

B. She is appreciating a painting.

C. She is picking up a handbag.

D. She is entering a museum.

正確答案為 B。

聽力測驗第一部分自本頁開始。

A. Question 1

Honey Bookstore

BUSINESS HOURS

MON	10:00	TO	21:00
TUE	Closed	TO	Closed
WED	10:00	TO	21:00
THU	10:00	TO	21:00
FRI	10:00	TO	21:00
SAT	9:00	TO	22:00
SUN	9:00	TO	22:00

第1回
第2回
第3回
第4回
第5回
第6回
第7回
第8回
第9回
第10回

B. Questions 2 and 3

Today

10 AM	Have brunch with Lisa
11 AM	
Noon	Watch a movie with Rosie
1 PM	
2 PM	
3 PM	Work out
4 PM	Knitting class
5 PM	
6 PM	
7 PM	Dine out
8 PM	

C. Questions 4 and 5

Jimmy's Diner
Menu

Combo A $10
Spaghetti + Drink

Combo B $20
Hamburger + Fries + Drink

Combo C $15
Fried Rice + Drink

Combo D $8
Cake + Drink

Drink Menu
Coffee (Americano/Latte) / Tea /
Juice* (Orange/Apple/Grape)
*Upgrade to juice for an extra $2

第二部分：問答

共 10 題，每題請聽光碟放音機播出一英語問句或直述句之後，從試題冊上 A、B、C、D 四個回答或回應中，選出一個最適合者作答。每題只播出一遍。

例：（聽）Now that we've come to Kenting, we should try water sports.
　　（看）A. You can try harder next time.
　　　　　B. Yes. I'm on the way there.
　　　　　C. That sounds exciting to me.
　　　　　D. We are coming in an hour.

正確答案為 C。

6. A. I drink coffee at home.
　　B. Why don't we check it out?
　　C. It really tastes very good.
　　D. Why not? Count me in.

7. A. You are really cold to me.
　　B. I am sick of everything.
　　C. I think I caught a cold.
　　D. I don't feel comfortable.

8. A. I don't feel secure here.
　　B. I'm still trying to find one.
　　C. I'm looking forward to it.
　　D. I didn't get what you mean.

9. A. Finally, his talents are being recognized.
　　B. I didn't know he's changing jobs.
　　C. He told me about the sales promotion.
　　D. Time management is very important.

10. A. Yes. I attended the anniversary.
　　B. Yes. It's a harvest festival.
　　C. No. I'm not interested in movies.
　　D. No. It didn't meet my expectation.

11. A. It's less convenient than driving a car.
    B. It takes concentration to ride.
    C. It's too crowded in the square.
    D. It contributes to climate change.

12. A. I really hate to take medicine.
    B. I realized I'm more into creative arts.
    C. Becoming a doctor has been my dream.
    D. It's a career that involves saving people.

13. A. I'm afraid I'm not very artistic.
    B. I feel awkward in front of a camera.
    C. Isn't it expensive to buy a photo?
    D. I'll give it a try to get fit.

14. A. I stayed up late on Christmas Eve.
    B. I played with fireworks with my cousins.
    C. My parents gave me red envelopes.
    D. It's usually during winter vacation.

15. A. It's so nice of you to address it.
    B. Great! I'll look for something else.
    C. Thanks. I feel great wearing it, too.
    D. Really? I thought blue suited me well.

第三部分：簡短對話

共 10 題，每題請聽光碟放音機播出一段對話及一個相關的問題後，從試題冊上 A、B、C、D 四個選項中選出一個最適合者作答。每段對話及問題只播出一遍。

例：（聽）（Woman） Excuse me. Does the next train go to the airport?

（Man） No. Actually, this is the high speed rail station. You should go to the airport MRT station nearby to get to the airport.

（Woman） Thank you for letting me know. This is my first time taking a train to the airport, so I didn't notice that.

Question: What happened to the woman?

（看） A. She missed her train.

B. She got on the wrong train.

C. She went to the wrong station.

D. Her flight has already left.

正確答案為 C。

16. A. Write his report.
    B. Fix the laptop.
    C. Report the problem online.
    D. Go to the maintenance department.

17. A. She is a productive novelist.
    B. She is famous worldwide.
    C. Her movies are worth seeing.
    D. She is very creative.

18. A. It will start next year.
    B. It was decided suddenly.
    C. Tony was admitted by multiple colleges.
    D. Tony has found a place to live.

19. A. She caught a cold.
    B. She had some spoiled food.
    C. She has a long-term health problem.
    D. She had to take sick leave from school.

20. A. Introduce some tea companies.
    B. Buy the man some tea.
    C. Recommend some kinds of wine.
    D. Go to Nantou with the man.

第1回
第2回
第3回
第4回
第5回
第6回
第7回
第8回
第9回
第10回

21. A. He only listens to pop songs.
     B. He mainly listens to domestic music.
     C. He does not listen to CDs.
     D. He buys albums to support musicians.

22. A. Introduce some souvenirs.
     B. Choose something in his place.
     C. Buy something for him.
     D. Try the cheesecake he bought.

23. A. Soft drinks.
     B. Potato chips.
     C. Milk.
     D. Ice cream.

24.

	TRAIN No.			
STATIONS	709	809	711	811
Oakmont	8:30	9:00	9:30	10:00
Sunnydale	|	9:23	|	10:23
Ashford	9:11	|	10:11	|
Rosewood	9:47	|	10:47	|
Davidtown	10:20	10:40	11:20	11:40

" | ": pass through

     A. Train No. 709.
     B. Train No. 809.
     C. Train No. 711.
     D. Train No. 811.

25.   **Jogging Shoes**

Model	M300	M500	S1000	S2000
Type	Basic	Basic	Advanced	Advanced
Cushioning	★	★★	★★	★★★
Light weight	★★	★	★★★	★★

     A. M300.
     B. M500.
     C. S1000.
     D. S2000.

第四部分：簡短談話

共 10 題，每題請聽光碟放音機播出一段談話及一個相關的問題後，從試題冊上 A、
B、C、D 四個選項中選出一個最適合者作答。每段談話及問題只播出一遍。

例： （聽）Teenagers can easily feel hurt in their social lives. When they have
difficulty making friends, they may feel worried about going to school.
Even if they are popular at school, they may be persuaded to do things
they don't like, such as smoking or drinking, under peer pressure. The
stress of fitting in can eventually make them mentally ill.

Question: According to the speaker, what makes a teenager try
smoking even though they are not interested?

（看）A. Parents' complaint.
B. Friends' persuasion.
C. Romantic relationship.
D. Academic pressure.

正確答案為 B。

26. A. To arrange a meet-up.
    B. To ask for a favor.
    C. To ask about train information.
    D. To confirm a reservation.

27. A. Process improvement.
    B. Performance evaluation.
    C. Cost reduction.
    D. Staff expansion.

28. A. Go to the dining car.
    B. Order in advance.
    C. Show their tickets.
    D. Wait for the service staff.

29. A. Midterm exam performance.
    B. Assignments.
    C. Class presentation.
    D. In-class interaction.

30. A. To find a person.
    B. To thank for recommending a
       service.
    C. To ask for medical care.
    D. To file a complaint.

31. A. A home appliance.
    B. A piece of furniture.
    C. A kitchen cabinet.
    D. A coffee mug.

32. A. A creative team.
    B. Product development.
    C. Advertising strategies.
    D. Foreign markets.

33. A. A traditional festival.
    B. A dance competition.
    C. A fireworks show.
    D. A musical event.

34.

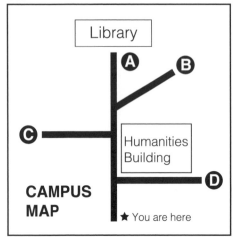

A. Location A.
B. Location B.
C. Location C.
D. Location D.

35.

Item	Price	Color
Floor lamp	$150	Gray, Black
Wall lamp	$120	Yellow, White, Blue
Table lamp	$90	White, Black
Bedside lamp	$70	Gray, Blue

A. The floor lamp.
B. The wall lamp.
C. The table lamp.
D. The bedside lamp.

本測驗分三部分，全為四選一之選擇題，共 35 題，作答時間 45 分鐘。

第一部分：詞彙

共 10 題，每題含一個空格。請由試題冊上的四個選項中選出最適合題意的字或詞作答。

1. It is hard to believe they are already celebrating their 10th _____. They still show a lot of affection for each other after so many years.
   - A. decade
   - B. demonstration
   - C. anniversary
   - D. achievement

2. Smoking causes _____ damage to your lungs, so its negative effects can persist even after quitting.
   - A. permanent
   - B. consistent
   - C. persuasive
   - D. productive

3. If you _____ with your colleagues, it is more likely they will support you when you face challenges.
   - A. go well
   - B. get along
   - C. put up
   - D. get away

4. The boss often assigns important tasks and projects to Peter because he is such a _____ person.
   - A. restless
   - B. resistant
   - C. reliable
   - D. relieved

5. Once you have set up your objectives, what you should do next is to think about how to _____ them.
   - A. surrender
   - B. overlook
   - C. motivate
   - D. fulfill

6. Jenna resembles her mother. She _____ her mother's big blue eyes and curly hair.
   A. inherited   B. acquired
   C. realized   D. exploited

7. This area of the factory is _____ guarded to keep out people who are not allowed.
   A. anxiously   B. vaguely
   C. passively   D. strictly

8. _____ insurance can help reduce the financial burden associated with hospital stays, surgeries, and other treatments.
   A. Mental   B. Medical
   C. Oral   D. Radical

9. Wearing face masks is a good way to prevent catching the flu because the virus can be _____ through the air.
   A. cultivated   B. extended
   C. commissioned   D. transmitted

10. The dance performance is _____ popular songs, making it easy to enjoy for a wide range of audience.
    A. demonstrated by   B. accompanied with
    C. eliminated to   D. identified as

第二部分：段落填空

共 10 題，包括二個段落，每個段落各含 5 個空格。請由試題冊上四個選項中選出最適合題意的字或詞作答。

Questions 11-15

Taylor Swift made music history in October 2022. __(11)__ the release of her tenth studio album, *Midnights*, Swift became the first artist to __(12)__ the entire top 10 on the Billboard Hot 100 chart. This achievement proves that she has an __(13)__ fan base. The secret to the continual increase of her fans lies in the songs she has created, which are mostly about relationships. Many people, especially young women, find her songs easy to __(14)__ . Swift is also famous for interacting with her fans in person, __(15)__ , further strengthening the bond between her and the community she has cultivated.

11. A. Regarding
     B. Following
     C. Considering
     D. Including

12. A. break into
     B. bring about
     C. take over
     D. drop behind

13. A. apparent
     B. efficient
     C. intense
     D. unconscious

14. A. relate to
     B. cheer up
     C. deal with
     D. hear about

15. A. causing confusion in society
     B. trying to get the best of them
     C. making them feel seen and valued
     D. reflecting the trend of social isolation

Questions 16-20

In the past, the ___(16)___ method of making a purchase was by using cash. However, since the ___(17)___ of credit and debit cards, people have grown to accept the concept of cashless payment. As technology continued to evolve, though, people started seeking more advanced payment methods ___(18)___ . This led to the development of mobile payment, which involves ___(19)___ value from one payment account to another using mobile devices, particularly smartphones.

___(20)___ its convenience, mobile payment is expected to play a major role in the future as the primary method of payment.

16. A. obvious
    B. singular
    C. financial
    D. sensitive

17. A. application
    B. convention
    C. introduction
    D. recognition

18. A. instead of paying by cash
    B. rather than relying on others
    C. beyond the use of plastic cards
    D. to get more rewards and
       benefits

19. A. translating
    B. transferring
    C. transporting
    D. transforming

20. A. Due to
    B. Except for
    C. In spite of
    D. By means of

第三部分：閱讀理解

共 15 題，包括數篇短文，每篇短文後有 2~4 個相關問題。請由試題冊上四個選項中選出最適合者作答。

Questions 21-22

From:	jennalin@greatagency.com
To:	helenchen@wondermusic.com
Subject:	Demo
Attachment:	kimmyklein_demo.zip

Dear Ms. Chen,

I am Jenna, a music agent from Great Agency, reaching out to recommend Kimmy Klein, our talented singer who recently won the Best New Artist award of this year. Kimmy has been writing songs since the age of 12 and has consistently received positive feedbacks for her work. Her music is known for its unique style and elegant lyrics, which I have attached for you to listen to. I would greatly appreciate your opinion on her talent. Thank you for your time.

Best Regards,

Jenna Lin
Music Agent
Great Agency

21. What is the intention of this email?
    A. To apply for a position
    B. To promote a new talent
    C. To introduce a new music trend
    D. To recommend someone for an award

22. What is true about Kimmy Klein?
    A. She is currently the most successful artist.
    B. She started making music as a child.
    C. She dresses with a unique style.
    D. She has not released any music yet.

Memo

Effective July, following the revised labor laws, employees working for more than four days in a row are required to take a day off before their next shift. Therefore, employees who have five work days in a row are required to exchange shifts with their colleagues under their managers' approval. To request a shift change, please access the company's internal website and find the "shift" page. On the right-hand side of the page, submit an application for the desired change, and you will receive an email confirming your application.

In addition, we have been receiving repeated complaints from customers about the poor service provided by certain clerks. Therefore, employees who have received three or more major complaints will be required to attend training at the headquarters. If you have any questions, please consult your managers.

23. Which of the following is **NOT** one of the purposes of this memo?
    A. To announce a new work schedule policy
    B. To explain how to apply for a shift change
    C. To bring employees' attention to customers' complaints
    D. To encourage the entire staff to attend training

24. What should employees do to change shifts?
    A. Apply online
    B. Talk to the executives
    C. Write an email
    D. Take sick leave

25. What does the training at the headquarters aim to improve?
    A. Sales techniques
    B. Time management
    C. Employee motivation
    D. Customer interactions

Questions 26-28 are based on information provided in the following notice and email.

Burgundy Café: Grand Opening!

Join us as we celebrate the opening of our 30th Burgundy Café branch! Since 2008, we have been committed to serving the finest coffee to our valued customers. Come and experience the exceptional flavors that have made us a hot spot for coffee lovers. Present the coupon below on February 28th to enjoy a 10% discount on all items. Moreover, Burgundy Café members enjoy a special 20% off on desserts on that day. We can't wait to serve you!

-10%

· Valid only on February 28, at the Blue Street branch of Burgundy Café
· Only one discount can be applied to each item

From:	jefflarison@dontlook.com
To:	customerservice@burgundycafe.com
Subject:	Error in discount application
Attachment:	receipt.jpg

To whom it may concern,

I am writing to bring to your attention an issue I encountered on the opening day of the new Burgundy Café on Blue Street. I purchased two cups of cappuccino and a sandwich, as you can see on the attached receipt. Despite presenting a coupon from your advertisement and my membership card, the clerk only applied a 10% discount instead of 20%. I kindly request your assistance in correcting this error by giving me back the 10% you have overcharged. Thank you for your attention to this matter.

Regards,
Jeff Larison

26. What is true about Burgundy Café?
    A. It is celebrating its 30th anniversary.
    B. It provided a one-day special offer.
    C. Its stores serve coffee only.
    D. It charges its members an annual fee.

27. Why did Mr. Larison send the email?
    A. To get some money back
    B. To confirm his order
    C. To renew his membership
    D. To complain about a clerk's attitude

28. What is the main reason that Mr. Larison only got a 10% discount instead of 20%?
    A. He went to a wrong location of Burgundy Café.
    B. His coupon was past due date.
    C. His purchase did not qualify for the higher discount.
    D. Different discounts cannot be combined.

第1回
第2回
第3回
第4回
第5回
第6回
第7回
第8回
第9回
第10回

One of the traditions of Chinese New Year is giving red envelopes to children. These envelopes filled with money symbolize good luck and wishes for the year ahead. Even though some only care about the money inside, red envelopes actually have deeper significance that most people do not notice.

According to folklore(民間傳說), a demon named "Sui(祟)" would scare children who are asleep on New Year's Eve. To protect them, parents would keep their children awake throughout the night. In one story, a boy was given eight coins to play with and stay awake, but eventually fell asleep, causing the coins to fall on his pillow. The boy was saved by the coins' powerful light, which frightened away the demon Sui. Therefore, the red envelope represents these protective coins and is known as "yasuiqian(壓歲錢)" or "suppressing Sui money". Today, this tradition has evolved to include gifting red envelopes to family, relatives, and friends, symbolizing the sharing of good luck.

29. What is this article mainly about?
    A. The proper way of giving red envelopes
    B. The meaning that red envelopes stand for
    C. The historical meaning of Chinese folklore
    D. The methods of attracting good luck

30. According to the article, what were red envelopes intended for in the very
    beginning?
    A. Protecting children from danger
    B. Earning fortune for the next year
    C. Teaching children how to use money
    D. Strengthening the bond within the family

31. According to the article, which of the following is **NOT** true?
    A. Red envelopes symbolize good luck and wishes.
    B. Not many people are aware of the deeper meaning of red envelopes.
    C. Children were advised to go to bed early on New Year's Eve in the past.
    D. People now give red envelopes not only to children but also to adults.

第1回
第2回
第3回
第4回
第5回
第6回
第7回
第8回
第9回
第10回

Are you addicted(上癮的) to social media? Do you experience anxiety when you are not using it? If so, you may be experiencing a phenomenon known as "FOMO", or the fear of missing out.

FOMO refers to the anxiety that arises when one feels they are missing out on information, experiences, events, or life decisions that could enhance their lives. It often comes from fear of regret and concerns about missing out on social interactions. If you find yourself constantly worrying about what others are doing, you might be dealing with FOMO.

The rise of social media has contributed to the spread of FOMO in recent years. As people spend more hours online, sharing their lives and comparing with others', they get more concerned that they may miss out some positive experiences while others seem to be making the most of their lives.

FOMO can also emerge outside social media. Brands looking to take advantage of it often employ "hunger marketing" techniques, such as providing limited stock or limiting the time that a product is available, creating a situation that urges consumers to buy as soon as possible. Consequently, consumers may end up buying things they neither need nor truly want in fear that stock will soon run out.

32. Which of the following best describes FOMO?
    A. Feeling regret for making some mistakes
    B. Being anxious about not meeting others' expectations
    C. Fearing that one's friends are talking behind their back
    D. Worrying about not experiencing something rewarding

33. Why does social media cause FOMO?
    A. It encourages us to share our feelings.
    B. It allows us to comment on social issues.
    C. It makes us compare our lives with others'.
    D. It makes finding our friends in real life easy.

34. According to this article, what is true about FOMO?
    A. It is a psychological phenomenon.
    B. It is considered a disease.
    C. It only happens on social media.
    D. It can damage consumer economy.

35. What is the aim of "hunger marketing"?
    A. Creating an urgent sense of desire
    B. Limiting the income generated by a product
    C. Communicating with consumers in a more sincere way
    D. Making a product popular across different consumer groups

第1回
第2回
第3回
第4回
第5回
第6回
第7回
第8回
第9回
第10回

第 1-2 回測驗答案紙

國際學村　全民英語能力分級檢定測驗　中級初試答案紙（第一回）

全民英語能力分級檢定測驗（第一回）

閱讀能力測驗

1	A B C D	21	A B C D		
2	A B C D	22	A B C D		
3	A B C D	23	A B C D		
4	A B C D	24	A B C D		
5	A B C D	25	A B C D		
6	A B C D	26	A B C D		
7	A B C D	27	A B C D		
8	A B C D	28	A B C D		
9	A B C D	29	A B C D		
10	A B C D	30	A B C D		
11	A B C D	31	A B C D		
12	A B C D	32	A B C D		
13	A B C D	33	A B C D		
14	A B C D	34	A B C D		
15	A B C D	35	A B C D		
16	A B C D				
17	A B C D				
18	A B C D				
19	A B C D				
20	A B C D				

聽力測驗

1	A B C D	21	A B C D
2	A B C D	22	A B C D
3	A B C D	23	A B C D
4	A B C D	24	A B C D
5	A B C D	25	A B C D
6	A B C D	26	A B C D
7	A B C D	27	A B C D
8	A B C D	28	A B C D
9	A B C D	29	A B C D
10	A B C D	30	A B C D
11	A B C D	31	A B C D
12	A B C D	32	A B C D
13	A B C D	33	A B C D
14	A B C D	34	A B C D
15	A B C D	35	A B C D
16	A B C D		
17	A B C D		
18	A B C D		
19	A B C D		
20	A B C D		

國際學村　全民英語能力分級檢定測驗　中級初試答案紙（第二回）

全民英語能力分級檢定測驗（第二回）

閱讀能力測驗

1	A B C D	21	A B C D
2	A B C D	22	A B C D
3	A B C D	23	A B C D
4	A B C D	24	A B C D
5	A B C D	25	A B C D
6	A B C D	26	A B C D
7	A B C D	27	A B C D
8	A B C D	28	A B C D
9	A B C D	29	A B C D
10	A B C D	30	A B C D
11	A B C D	31	A B C D
12	A B C D	32	A B C D
13	A B C D	33	A B C D
14	A B C D	34	A B C D
15	A B C D	35	A B C D
16	A B C D		
17	A B C D		
18	A B C D		
19	A B C D		
20	A B C D		

聽力測驗

1	A B C D	21	A B C D
2	A B C D	22	A B C D
3	A B C D	23	A B C D
4	A B C D	24	A B C D
5	A B C D	25	A B C D
6	A B C D	26	A B C D
7	A B C D	27	A B C D
8	A B C D	28	A B C D
9	A B C D	29	A B C D
10	A B C D	30	A B C D
11	A B C D	31	A B C D
12	A B C D	32	A B C D
13	A B C D	33	A B C D
14	A B C D	34	A B C D
15	A B C D	35	A B C D
16	A B C D		
17	A B C D		
18	A B C D		
19	A B C D		
20	A B C D		

第 3-4 回測驗答案紙

國際學村 全民英語能力分級檢定測驗 中級初試答案紙（第四回）

閱讀能力測驗

聽力測驗

國際學村 全民英語能力分級檢定測驗 中級初試答案紙（第三回）

閱讀能力測驗

聽力測驗

第 5-6 回測驗答案紙

國際學村　全民英語能力分級檢定測驗　中級初試答案紙（第六回）

閱讀能力測驗

#	A B C D	#	A B C D
1	A B C D	21	A B C D
2	A B C D	22	A B C D
3	A B C D	23	A B C D
4	A B C D	24	A B C D
5	A B C D	25	A B C D
6	A B C D	26	A B C D
7	A B C D	27	A B C D
8	A B C D	28	A B C D
9	A B C D	29	A B C D
10	A B C D	30	A B C D
11	A B C D	31	A B C D
12	A B C D	32	A B C D
13	A B C D	33	A B C D
14	A B C D	34	A B C D
15	A B C D	35	A B C D
16	A B C D		
17	A B C D		
18	A B C D		
19	A B C D		
20	A B C D		

聽力測驗

#	A B C D	#	A B C D
1	A B C D	21	A B C D
2	A B C D	22	A B C D
3	A B C D	23	A B C D
4	A B C D	24	A B C D
5	A B C D	25	A B C D
6	A B C D	26	A B C D
7	A B C D	27	A B C D
8	A B C D	28	A B C D
9	A B C D	29	A B C D
10	A B C D	30	A B C D
11	A B C D	31	A B C D
12	A B C D	32	A B C D
13	A B C D	33	A B C D
14	A B C D	34	A B C D
15	A B C D	35	A B C D
16	A B C D		
17	A B C D		
18	A B C D		
19	A B C D		
20	A B C D		

國際學村　全民英語能力分級檢定測驗　中級初試答案紙（第五回）

閱讀能力測驗

#	A B C D	#	A B C D
1	A B C D	21	A B C D
2	A B C D	22	A B C D
3	A B C D	23	A B C D
4	A B C D	24	A B C D
5	A B C D	25	A B C D
6	A B C D	26	A B C D
7	A B C D	27	A B C D
8	A B C D	28	A B C D
9	A B C D	29	A B C D
10	A B C D	30	A B C D
11	A B C D	31	A B C D
12	A B C D	32	A B C D
13	A B C D	33	A B C D
14	A B C D	34	A B C D
15	A B C D	35	A B C D
16	A B C D		
17	A B C D		
18	A B C D		
19	A B C D		
20	A B C D		

聽力測驗

#	A B C D	#	A B C D
1	A B C D	21	A B C D
2	A B C D	22	A B C D
3	A B C D	23	A B C D
4	A B C D	24	A B C D
5	A B C D	25	A B C D
6	A B C D	26	A B C D
7	A B C D	27	A B C D
8	A B C D	28	A B C D
9	A B C D	29	A B C D
10	A B C D	30	A B C D
11	A B C D	31	A B C D
12	A B C D	32	A B C D
13	A B C D	33	A B C D
14	A B C D	34	A B C D
15	A B C D	35	A B C D
16	A B C D		
17	A B C D		
18	A B C D		
19	A B C D		
20	A B C D		

第 7-8 回測驗答案紙

第 9-10 回測驗答案紙

第十回

國際學村

全民英語能力分級檢定測驗
中級初試答案紙（第十回）

聽力測驗

題號	A	B	C	D
1	A	B	C	D
2	A	B	C	D
3	A	B	C	D
4	A	B	C	D
5	A	B	C	D
6	A	B	C	D
7	A	B	C	D
8	A	B	C	D
9	A	B	C	D
10	A	B	C	D
11	A	B	C	D
12	A	B	C	D
13	A	B	C	D
14	A	B	C	D
15	A	B	C	D
16	A	B	C	D
17	A	B	C	D
18	A	B	C	D
19	A	B	C	D
20	A	B	C	D
21	A	B	C	D
22	A	B	C	D
23	A	B	C	D
24	A	B	C	D
25	A	B	C	D
26	A	B	C	D
27	A	B	C	D
28	A	B	C	D
29	A	B	C	D
30	A	B	C	D
31	A	B	C	D
32	A	B	C	D
33	A	B	C	D
34	A	B	C	D
35	A	B	C	D

閱讀能力測驗

題號	A	B	C	D
1	A	B	C	D
2	A	B	C	D
3	A	B	C	D
4	A	B	C	D
5	A	B	C	D
6	A	B	C	D
7	A	B	C	D
8	A	B	C	D
9	A	B	C	D
10	A	B	C	D
11	A	B	C	D
12	A	B	C	D
13	A	B	C	D
14	A	B	C	D
15	A	B	C	D
16	A	B	C	D
17	A	B	C	D
18	A	B	C	D
19	A	B	C	D
20	A	B	C	D
21	A	B	C	D
22	A	B	C	D
23	A	B	C	D
24	A	B	C	D
25	A	B	C	D
26	A	B	C	D
27	A	B	C	D
28	A	B	C	D
29	A	B	C	D
30	A	B	C	D
31	A	B	C	D
32	A	B	C	D
33	A	B	C	D
34	A	B	C	D
35	A	B	C	D

第九回

國際學村

全民英語能力分級檢定測驗
中級初試答案紙（第九回）

聽力測驗

題號	A	B	C	D
1	A	B	C	D
2	A	B	C	D
3	A	B	C	D
4	A	B	C	D
5	A	B	C	D
6	A	B	C	D
7	A	B	C	D
8	A	B	C	D
9	A	B	C	D
10	A	B	C	D
11	A	B	C	D
12	A	B	C	D
13	A	B	C	D
14	A	B	C	D
15	A	B	C	D
16	A	B	C	D
17	A	B	C	D
18	A	B	C	D
19	A	B	C	D
20	A	B	C	D
21	A	B	C	D
22	A	B	C	D
23	A	B	C	D
24	A	B	C	D
25	A	B	C	D
26	A	B	C	D
27	A	B	C	D
28	A	B	C	D
29	A	B	C	D
30	A	B	C	D
31	A	B	C	D
32	A	B	C	D
33	A	B	C	D
34	A	B	C	D
35	A	B	C	D

閱讀能力測驗

題號	A	B	C	D
1	A	B	C	D
2	A	B	C	D
3	A	B	C	D
4	A	B	C	D
5	A	B	C	D
6	A	B	C	D
7	A	B	C	D
8	A	B	C	D
9	A	B	C	D
10	A	B	C	D
11	A	B	C	D
12	A	B	C	D
13	A	B	C	D
14	A	B	C	D
15	A	B	C	D
16	A	B	C	D
17	A	B	C	D
18	A	B	C	D
19	A	B	C	D
20	A	B	C	D
21	A	B	C	D
22	A	B	C	D
23	A	B	C	D
24	A	B	C	D
25	A	B	C	D
26	A	B	C	D
27	A	B	C	D
28	A	B	C	D
29	A	B	C	D
30	A	B	C	D
31	A	B	C	D
32	A	B	C	D
33	A	B	C	D
34	A	B	C	D
35	A	B	C	D